ADORING ALI & ACE

PEPPER NORTH

Text copyright© 2020 Pepper North
All Rights Reserved

Dr. Richards' Littles®
is a registered trademark of
With A Wink Publishing, LLC.
All rights reserved.

AUTHOR'S NOTE:

The following story is completely fictional. The characters are all over the age of 18 and as adults choose to live their lives in an age play environment. This is a series of books that can be read in any order. You may, however, choose to read them sequentially to enjoy the characters best. Subsequent books will feature characters that appear in previous novels as well as new faces.

AN INVITATION TO BE PART OF PEPPER'S LITTLES LEAGUE!

Want to read more stories featuring Zoey and all the Littles? Join Pepper North's newsletter. Every other issue will include a short story as well as other fun features! She promises not to overwhelm your mailbox and you can unsubscribe at any time.

As a special bonus, Pepper will send you a free collection of three short stories to get you started on all the Littles' fun activities!

Here's the link:

http://BookHip.com/FJBPQV

OTHER TITLES BY PEPPER NORTH

Zoey: Dr. Richards' Littles® 1

Amy: Dr. Richards' Littles® 2

Carrie: Dr. Richards' Littles® 3

Jake: Dr. Richards' Littles® 4

Angelina: Dr. Richards' Littles® 5

Brad: Dr. Richards' Littles® 6

The Digestive Health Center: Susan's Story

Charlotte: Dr. Richards' Littles® 7

Sofia and Isabella: Dr. Richards' Littles® 8

Cecily: Dr. Richards' Littles® 9

Tony: Dr. Richards' Littles® 10

The Keepers: Payi

Abigail: Dr. Richards' Littles® 11

Madi: Dr. Richards' Littles® 12

Penelope: Dr. Richards' Littles® 13

Christmas with the Littles & Wendy: Dr. Richards' Littles® 14

Olivia: Dr. Richards' Littles® 15

Matty & Emma: Dr. Richards' Littles® 16

The Magic of Twelve: Violet

Fiona: Dr. Richards' Littles® 17

The Keepers: Pien

Oliver: Dr. Richards' Littles® 18

The Magic of Twelve: Marigold

Luna: Dr. Richards' Littles® 19

Lydia & Neil: Dr. Richards' Littles® 20

A Little Vacation South of the Border

The Magic of Twelve: Hazel

Roxy: Dr. Richards' Littles® 21

Dr. Richards' Littles®: First Anniversary Collection

Jillian: Dr. Richards' Littles® 22

The Magic of Twelve: Sienna

Hunter: Dr. Richards' Littles® 23

Sharing Shelby: A SANCTUM Novel

The Magic of Twelve: Pearl

Dr. Richards' Littles®: MM Collection

Electrostatic Bonds

Grace: Dr. Richards' Littles® 24

Looking After Lindy: A SANCTUM Novel

The Keepers: Naja

Tales from Zoey's Corner - ABC

Steven: Dr. Richards' Littles® 25

The Magic of Twelve: Violet, Marigold, Hazel

The Magic of Twelve: Primrose

The Keepers Collection

Protecting Priscilla: A SANCTUM Novel

One Sweet Treat: A SANCTUM Novel

The Magic of Twelve: Sky

Tales from Zoey's Corner - DEF

Sylvie: Dr. Richards' Littles® 26

Tami: Dr. Richards' Littles® 27

Liam: Dr. Richards' Littles® 28

Dr. Richards' Littles®: 2nd Anniversary Collection

Picking Poppy: A SANCTUM Novel

The Magic of Twelve: Amber

Tim: Dr. Richards' Littles® 29

Tales From Zoey's Corner - GHI

Once Upon A Time: A Dr. Richards' Littles® Story

Rescuing Rita: A SANCTUM Novel

The Magic of Twelve: Indigo

Tales From Zoey's Corner - JKL

Tales From Zoey's Corner - MNO

Needing Nicky: A SANCTUM Novel

Tales From Zoey's Corner - PQR

Serena: Dr. Richards' Littles® 30

The Medic's Littles Girl

The Magic of Twelve: Rose

Tales From Zoey's Corner - W, X, Y, Z

Tales From Zoey's Corner - A-Z

Sophie: Dr. Richards' Littles® 31

3rd Anniversary Collection

Adoring Ali & Ace: A SANCTUM Novel

Tex's Little Girl

Marked Brides

CHAPTER 1

"Yes, sir. The electronic trail leads directly back to Mr. Miller's personal computer," Zeke Clark confirmed. Looking at the defense attorney frantically scribbling notes for his cross-examination, Zeke schooled his features to hide his internal glee. The amount of illegal porn that he had found both on Mr. Miller's laptop and in the cloud had fueled his efforts to create an irrefutable case.

Ninety minutes later, Zeke walked out of the preceding room. He rolled his shoulders back to release the tension in his muscles. Court was the least favorite part of his job. Thank goodness he didn't have to appear often. When Zeke did testify, the evidence only he could produce helped lock up dangerous felons.

Walking out into the fresh summer air, he celebrated his decision to relocate to SANCTUM. He'd been planning this for months. Dividing his time between the gated community and his thriving business, Zeke had finally admitted to himself that his heart was there and not in the city.

All I need is to find my Little, or Littles. Although it seemed selfish to dream of having two Littles, Zeke had always been sure that his destiny was linked with a Little boy and Little girl. He just had to find them.

Zeke slid behind the wheel of his large SUV and headed back to the hotel. One more night, and he would be off. He was taking a vacation for the first time in years before heading back to SANCTUM. The builders had almost completed his home there.

After making a complete break with his previous life in the city, Zeke had sold his house and furniture. The new family moved in three days ago. He'd stayed in town only to finish up the court case. With Mr. Miller on his way to jail for fifteen years, Zeke would check out of the hotel he'd called home for the last week.

Zeke followed his GPS to the small coastal town where he had rented a house for two weeks. The distance away would help him transition and relax from the stress of his job. Now with the window down, the salty scent of the ocean filled his mind with pleasant memories. As he passed businesses advertising surfboards for rent, Zeke wondered if riding the waves was the same as riding a bike. He'd been pretty good in his twenties. Would he remember all the skills?

"Yeah. I'm so going to get a board," he admitted to himself, feeling his lips curve in a satisfied grin.

A seafood restaurant packed with patrons caught his eye. Without a second thought, Zeke pulled into the lot and found a space. If this many people enjoyed the fare here, he would try it. Perhaps there would be room at the bar for one more hungry diner?

Sliding onto the barstool, Zeke looked around and celebrated his luck in finding an open seat. He opened the menu and scanned the delicious-sounding entrées. The cheerful voice made him look up.

"Hi, sir! Can I get you something to drink?" The cute brunette wore a T-shirt bearing the logo of the restaurant. Her smile was friendly and bright.

Reading her name tag, Zeke returned the greeting. "Hi, Ali! I'm going to put myself in your hands. What's the best thing on the menu?"

Her grin intensified. Bouncing enthusiastically on her toes, Ali rushed to assure him, "You want the fish and chips. I know it sounds boring, but wait until you taste it."

"I'll take it. You wouldn't lead me astray," he replied with confidence. "What am I having to drink?"

"We have a local ale that's tasty."

"Sold. Thanks, Ali."

In a flash, she was back with a chilled mug of the pale concoction. Ali hovered as he took his first sip. "Mmmm. This is perfect," he confirmed.

A tanned young man appeared at Ali's side to lean over the bar. "Ali will make that brewery famous all by herself." He laughed and nudged the young woman with his elbow.

"Ace, don't you have something to do at your end of the bar?" she asked with a laugh.

"Shh! I can't help it if you have all the fun people at your end." Ace extended a hand to Zeke. "Hi, I'm Ace."

Shaking the hand of the enthusiastic young man, Zeke laughed, "That's a lot of pressure to put on me."

"You can handle it," Ace replied with spunk. A patron at the other end of the bar signaled for a refill by lifting his glass. "Duty calls."

"I'll go get your food. Here's something to protect yourself with if Ace comes back again," Ali suggested, laying a plastic cocktail sword in front of him on the bar.

Unable to stop himself, Zeke laughed. He watched Ali bounce away. Glancing at Ace, he discovered the young man watching him. Nodding his way, Zeke picked up the small pink skewer and brandished it. To his delight, Ace immediately armed himself with a blue one. Their epic air sword fight only ended when Ali returned with his fish and chips.

Abandoning the game to sample the hot treat in front of him, Zeke groaned with delight. So good! He flashed a thumbs-up sign to Ali, who hovered in front of him. She clapped her hands in delight before rushing to help a couple two stools down with fancy frozen drinks.

The bustling crowd kept Zeke from chatting with either bartender. There was something about them that drew his attention. It wasn't only their fun-loving spirit. To his amazement, the pair managed the packed bar with grace, humor, and skill. Zeke tried to convince himself that he was imagining it, but neither one interacted so personally with other guests as they had with him. He was pleased to find their eyes on him often.

He enjoyed the meal Ali had recommended and settled his bill.

Leaving her a generous tip, he slid from the stool. Before moving away, Zeke picked up the pink cocktail sword. *You never know when you'll need one of these.* Waving at both bartenders, he answered their urges for him to come back soon. "I'll look forward to seeing you again." As he walked out the door, Zeke realized that he meant it. He hoped to see them soon.

With one last stop before he drove to the house he had rented, Zeke pulled into a surf shop on the edge of town. It wasn't painted brightly or fancy like the ones on the strip. Walking in, a man and a toddler who was obviously his granddaughter greeted him. The older man scooped up the baby girl in a pink tutu before asking, "Are you looking for a souvenir?"

"I'm here for a couple weeks. I used to be pretty good back in my twenties," Zeke explained. "I don't suppose you have any boards for rent?"

"Where are you staying?"

Zeke knew it was a test. "I've rented Fred Tucker's place on Seashore Lane."

"It would tickle Fred to know a fellow surfer rented his place. You all alone?"

"Unfortunately." He held up his hands as if warding off trouble. "Don't worry. I'm too old to have rocking parties. I'm just here to relax while they finish my house."

The man's smile widened. "I know what you say about being too old. I have to get my beauty sleep so I can take care of my princess here. I don't normally rent boards, but I have one here that my boy uses when he's home from the Navy. I'll be glad to loan it to you."

"I'll insist on paying you. If you're sure your son wouldn't mind, I'll take you up on that offer," Zeke answered, holding out one hand.

With a shake, they determined a price. Zeke learned the shopkeeper's name was Abe, and he'd lived there all his life. As Zeke tied the board on the top of his SUV with skilled practice, he realized how much he missed surfing. As he said his goodbyes to Abe and his granddaughter, Ashley, the older man handed him a tube of liniment.

"You'll need this in a couple of days," he predicted. "Come back if you need any supplies."

CHAPTER 2

The next morning, Zeke woke up in an unfamiliar bed. It had a few lumps and bumps but felt better than his expensive mattress did in his high-rise apartment. He'd slept like a log with the sea breezes blowing in the open window.

Too bad SANCTUM wasn't by the sea. Little girls and boys would love to play in the sand. He'd have to remember this place. There would be plenty of room for a family to vacation here.

Forcing himself out of bed, Zeke appreciated the filled kitchen he had arranged to have stocked for his arrival. He looked out the kitchen window as he filled up the coffeepot. It was an easy decision to have breakfast out on the deck. *Who doesn't like scrambled eggs with a view of the ocean?*

Not able to be a complete hermit, Zeke connected his computer to the Wi-Fi using the password which the rental company had messaged him. Expecting the connection to be slow, Zeke was delighted to find the bandwidth allowed him to operate at normal speed. After checking for urgent messages, he decided that everything else could wait. The beach was calling his name.

Stepping into a pair of long swim trunks and a sun shirt, Zeke slathered himself in sunscreen. He wouldn't stay long, but he didn't want to go back to Abe's in a couple of hours looking for aloe vera gel to soothe the sunburn. Hoisting the board, Zeke balanced it under one arm as he headed down the stairs to the sand. In three minutes, he was thigh-deep in the water. With joyful glee, he jumped onto the waxed board and began paddling.

Several surfers were already in the water. They greeted him with waves and shouted words. Zeke was careful to move to an area away from most. He didn't want to get in their way or hurt anyone.

Instinct kicked in. When the perfect wave lifted his surfboard, Zeke jumped to standing and began to ride the water. It felt good. A perfect ride wasn't quite the most honest description, but he was tickled when he stayed upright for several minutes. After crashing into the water, Zeke burst above the surface and immediately began laughing. *What a rush!*

"Hey! For an old man, you did pretty well," a familiar voice called from behind him.

Zeke turned to see Ali and Ace seated atop their boards. "Hey, you two!" Sliding up to lie on his stomach on the board, Zeke paddled his arms to reach them. He sat up, and Ace automatically tethered his board to theirs by stretching a leg over the nose of Zeke's board.

"I may feel like an old man tomorrow, but I feel about your age while I'm riding. I forgot how much I miss this," he shared. "Do you two surf every morning?"

"Most days," Ali answered with a bright smile. "We miss this if we're assigned to work the lunch crowd. Today is actually our day off. We'll surf for another hour. Then, if I can talk Ace into building a sandcastle with me, we'll work on that. He's incredibly talented."

"I'll let you get back to enjoying your day off," Zeke said.

"Don't you want to have fun with us?" Ali asked. Her typically animated face looked sad.

"I'd love to hang with the natives if you don't mind an old guy," he joked.

"Hooray!" Ali cheered. She held up a hand to Ace, who smacked it with enthusiasm. "Let's go!"

Stretching out on his board again, Zeke followed the young couple. *They seem to know exactly where the waves would begin.*

With their guidance, Zeke channeled his younger talent and regained some skills. He couldn't compete with Ali and Ace, but he didn't feel like he was holding them back too much.

That one hour Ali had planned stretched into two before they all turned toward the shore. The water was filling with more novice riders, and Zeke's muscles were starting to burn. Knowing that he would feel this tomorrow, Zeke had agreed that it was time to stop.

"I'm starving!" Ace declared as they carried their boards up the beach. He upended his board in the sand before taking Ali's and placing it in front of his. Zeke followed suit and earned the highest commendation— a thumbs-up from Ace. He dropped to the round blanket that Ali spread over the sand.

"That was a blast! I'd forgotten how much I enjoyed surfing," Zeke shared.

"You're pretty good for a rusty old guy," Ace joked.

Without thinking, Zeke reacted like a Daddy. "Don't make me spank you for being a brat."

Both Ali and Ace stared at him in disbelief. Immediately, Zeke covered his mistake. "Just kidding, of course! You're a grown man. I wouldn't spank you," Zeke laughed almost naturally.

"For a minute there, you sounded like my Daddy," Ace mumbled.

"Sorry to ruin the fun. I'll get going so the two of you can make your sandcastle and enjoy this beautiful day." Zeke rose to his feet and walked over to pluck his rented board out of the lineup. With a wave, he began walking down the beach. With each step, he berated himself for responding as he would normally at SANCTUM. "You've got to remember. This isn't SANCTUM!" he reminded himself.

"Hey! What's SANCTUM?" Ali appeared from behind to walk along the soft sand with Zeke.

"It's the community where I'm building my home. Sorry, I screwed things up," Zeke apologized again. He stopped and looked at Ali. "I enjoyed hanging out with you and Ace. I hope you let me surf with you again if we end up out here at the same time."

"You didn't screw anything up. I'm sorry we didn't react better. You surprised us. I have extra peanut butter and jelly sandwiches and some bottles of water. Won't you come back and have lunch with us?" Ali asked, shifting her weight from one foot to another as if nervous.

"Are you sure Ace is okay with me returning?"

Ali giggled. "He's the one that sent me. Come on!" Playfully, she ran around him to push one end of the board, turning him back toward the blanket. Linking her arm with his free one, she urged him forward.

Her laughter was contagious. It was also irresistible. Zeke allowed her to steer him back to where Ace waited. After replacing his surfboard in the sand, Zeke dropped to the blanket. The moment he was settled, Ace launched forward to wrap him in a brief hug. He moved away before Zeke could wrap an arm around him.

As Zeke tried to figure out what was happening, Ali handed out the sandwiches. She'd spread peanut butter thickly over the plain white bread and added globs of grape jelly. Suddenly, he was ravenous for the simple treat. "Thanks, Ali!"

They all bit into the sandwiches. Mmms filled the air. When Zeke polished his off in record time, Ali laid another sandwich in front of him. "Oh, I can't eat all your food. One sandwich will hold me. I'm trying to watch my waistline," Zeke joked.

"We've got plenty. And you're not pudgy," Ace reassured him, before starting his third sandwich.

Zeke smiled at him. He remembered those days when he inhaled food. He noticed Ali looking at the sandwiches. Guessing that she was trying to decide whether to eat a second, he picked up the one in front of him. "Ali, let's split this one," he suggested, unwrapping the plastic wrap and pulling out the sandwich. When she nodded enthusiastically, he carefully tore the sandwich almost in half and handed her the bigger part.

He enjoyed watching her wiggle in delight on the blanket as she nibbled on the second half. *Damn!* Why couldn't he find a duo like this who was Little and needed a Daddy? Zeke shook that thought from his mind. He would simply enjoy their company.

"I don't suppose I could return the favor and provide lunch tomorrow?" Zeke asked, leaning backward slightly.

"We both work the lunch shift tomorrow. We won't have time to come surf. But we're working during dinner the next day. Would you like to surf then?" Ace asked.

"It's a date. I'll bring lunch. Now, did somebody say something about building a sandcastle?" he asked.

"Woohoo! I've got everything we need," Ali professed. From an enormous bag, she began pulling out a variety of forms and tools.

Immediately, they created an intricate castle. With multiple trips down to the shore for water, they crafted shapes with the wet sand and contoured it. Shoulder to shoulder, they leaned over the collaborative project. With each contact, Zeke met Ace or Ali's eyes. He could feel the heat beginning to build between them as shy smiles and more deliberate bumps emerged as they worked together.

Zeke felt their eyes on his body as they studied him. Their interest was not casual. Turning his head as Ace approached with a new pail of water, Zeke traced the younger man's gaze to his ass displayed by his position on all fours. When Ace realized Zeke had caught him staring, his face turned beet red.

"Sorry," he mumbled as he dropped to his knees next to Zeke.

Rising to his knees to be eye to eye with Ace, Zeke wrapped an arm around his waist and pulled Ace against his side. "I'm not offended." His sandy hand slid down to cup one of Ace's taut buttocks for a brief moment before dropping his arm. "I'm having a tough time keeping my hands on the castle. I'm controlling myself because of our audience," he explained, nodding at the other beach visitors.

"Hey, what about me?" Ali joked, nudging Zeke from the other side. "I don't have a sandy print on my bottom," she pointed out. Ace looked over his shoulder as Zeke turned to check out Ace's beach shorts. Clear as day, a scattering of shiny grains formed a hand on one buttock.

"My apologies, Little one," Zeke said. "May I?" he asked. At her delighted giggle and nod, he pressed his palm against her small bottom.

An exchanged glance between his new friends warned Zeke what was coming. Soon his swim trucks had sandy prints emblazoned on them as well. His penis stirred at their touch. Playful but intimate, Ali and Ace weren't just friends on the beach anymore. He now knew they were interested in him, just as they drew him on a much deeper level.

Zeke turned back to the sandcastle as he tried to settle his jumbled thoughts and emotions. After all this time searching for his Littles, could he have found them here on vacation? He forced his attention back to the project in front of him. The trio's conversation lightened as if everyone focused on fun rather than their brewing attraction. Joking as they messed something up and celebrating when a feature came to life, the trio captured the attention of other beachgoers.

"Hey! That looks amazing! Are you all professionals?" a dad called as he stood a short distance away, holding both of his sons' hands to keep them from running forward to help.

"Ace is," Ali whispered beside Zeke.

"We have a specialist working with us today." He gestured to Ace.

The attention of the spectators immediately gravitated to the young man. Ace stood and turned to the audience. He answered several questions. Zeke loved that he encouraged the children to start small and practice. When the crowd faded away, he returned to kneel at Zeke's side.

"Thanks, man," he whispered to Zeke.

"They can all see where the actual talent lies. It's not in my hands. So tell me, boss, what should we do to that section." He pointed to a large mound that they had not yet decorated. Listening carefully to Ace's descriptions, he and Ali moved to begin the preliminary work. The expert craftsman remained where he was doing last touches.

"Ace never gets credit for his skills. Thanks for giving him that," Ali softly commented.

"Thanks for clueing me in." Zeke smiled at her.

The trio worked quietly side by side for several minutes. The sun felt good on his shoulders. He couldn't remember how long it had been since he'd done something as creative and random as building a sandcastle. It seemed like he'd known Ali and Ace for much longer than one meal and a morning at the beach. Their conversation was definitely enjoyable. These two were a delight.

"Ali, could you show me where you stored our keys in the basket?"

Ace asked. When Ali opened her mouth to tell him, Ace interrupted, "You know I can't find anything in that basket. Will you help me?"

Looking confused, Ali stood and followed Ace to their blanket a short distance away. He dropped to his knees in front of the basket and drew her down beside him. They bent their heads over the wicker container.

Zeke glanced over and noticed no one opened it. He smiled at the scene. Ali's brunette hair captured in a messy ponytail almost touched Ace's closely cropped, sun-bleached blond hair. They were an enchanting pair. Each totally different from the other, but yet somehow similar. Ace was a fun-loving daredevil and often challenging. His opposite, Ali, was sweet and wished to please. They meshed well together.

He knew that they weren't looking for keys. Ace wanted to tell Ali something privately. *I guess I'll see that they're ready to ditch me if they come back and make some excuse to leave.* There was nothing he could do but wait and see what they revealed.

"I love what you're doing for the brick in the castle wall," Ali said as she dropped to her knees beside him.

Zeke studied her face, looking for a clue about the conversation. She looked nervous. Taking a deep breath, Zeke said, "You tell me when you're ready to head off the beach. I know you have a lot of things to do on your day off."

"This is our favorite thing to do. We're enjoying hanging out with you," Ace said in a rush.

A companionable silence grew between them as they worked on different parts of the castle walls. Zeke finished the brick effect on the space in front of him. As he shifted over to work next to Ace, the young man continued to shape the sand in front of him.

"So, are you…"

"Are you married…?"

Zeke and Ace spoke at the same time. The trio laughed before Zeke answered. "I'm not married now. A conventional relationship is not what I'm looking for as a life partner. How about you all? Have you been dating long?"

Ali looked at Ace before answering. When he nodded, she turned her blue eyes to Zeke. "Ace and I have known each other since we were kids. We have one of those unconventional relationships. We're together, but our relationship isn't complete."

She stopped to confirm with Ace that she should continue. He nodded once again. Taking a deep breath, Ali confessed, "We're looking for a Daddy."

"When you mentioned spanking, we think maybe… Are you a Daddy?" Ace asked with a guarded expression.

Zeke looked at them seriously, "Do you know what you're talking about?"

Ali rushed to add, "We're pretty sure they exist. We've read about them in books. If you're not one, sorry. I hope you're not offended that we asked?"

"Littles exist, thank goodness. I have been searching for my Littles for years. My new home will be complete in two weeks in a gated community called SANCTUM. SANCTUM only exists for those who practice age play," Zeke shared.

"You said Littles, as in more than one." Ace looked at him speculatively.

"I did. I've known from the beginning that I was searching for two Littles—a Little boy and a Little girl. I would have never dreamed that I'd find what I was looking for on vacation. Would you like to get out of here? Go somewhere less sandy and more private?" Zeke suggested.

"I'd like that," Ali answered happily.

Ace chimed in, "Me, too."

"I'm staying in the house up there," Zeke pointed back to the home he had rented. "We don't have to go inside if you're not comfortable. There's an extensive deck that looks out on the ocean."

Ace looked over at two kids around ten or eleven years old. Obviously a brother and sister, they had been watching the construction process from a distance the entire time the trio had been working. "Hey! We have to leave. Would you finish the castle for us?"

Instantly, they nodded and rushed forward. "Really? Can we?"

"It's all yours," Ali said, rising to her feet. She held her hand out to Zeke to help him up. When he was on his feet, Ali didn't release his fingers. Instead, she intertwined hers with his.

Zeke turned to hold his hand out to Ace, standing nearby. With a lurch forward, Ace gripped it fiercely, as if he was afraid Zeke would disappear. "I'm not going anywhere until we figure this out," he whispered to the young man.

"Promise?"

"I promise you both."

CHAPTER 3

Quickly, the trio gathered all the sculpting tools and pails, shook the sand from the blanket, and gathered their belongings. Ace and Ali lined up to carry a surfboard under each arm together. One took the forward spot, and the other held the back of the boards. Zeke lifted his board and tucked it under one arm before leaning down to pick up the basket.

Heavily laden, they walked a short distance to Zeke's home away from home. Stowing the boards in the rack provided at the edge of the deck, Zeke asked, "Shall we talk inside or outside?"

"Could I use your bathroom?" Ali asked nervously.

"Let's all go in." Zeke opened the back door and gestured for everyone to precede him.

"This is nice," Ace observed.

Watching Ali dance in place, Zeke put a hand low on her spine and guided her to the hallway. "It's the second door on the left." When she almost ran to the door, Zeke felt his lips curve in amusement. Turning to Ace, he asked, "She doesn't like to go to the bathroom in the ocean, huh?"

"She feels like she's peeing on the fish," Ace laughed.

"I never looked at it like that. Let me get some towels and spread them on the couch. Then our sandy swimsuits won't leave an impression on the fabric," Zeke instructed.

As he turned to walk down the hall, Ace asked, "Do you really want a Little boy? It's okay if you've been looking for a Little girl only."

Turning, Zeke could read the uncertainty written in Ace's expression. He walked to stand in front of the younger man. "I am attracted to both males and females, Ace. While many Daddies treasure Little girls above all, I knew that I would need two Littles when I began my search. I assure you I have enough love for you both. May I touch you, Ace?"

At the younger man's nod, Zeke stepped forward and wrapped his hand around the back of Ace's head. Pulling him forward, Zeke pressed his lips against the Little's. Two seconds later, Ace leaned forward into the kiss as his arms wrapped around Zeke's waist. Controlling the kiss, Zeke explored the young man's mouth. He enjoyed the sweet sounds that came from deep inside Ace.

When Zeke heard a soft gasp from behind, he lifted his head. Whispering, he told Ace, "I searched for you just as hard as I looked for my Little girl."

Ace's eyes filled with hope. "Really?"

Zeke turned slightly and held the other hand for Ali to join them. Eagerly, she stepped forward to hear Zeke's assurance. "I will always be totally honest with both of you."

He pulled her into his arms. Zeke noticed Ace and Ali automatically wrapped an arm around each other. The level of love that tied the two young people together was palpable. Was it too much to hope for? Could these two actually be his Littles? He knew they were asking themselves the same questions.

"Would... would you kiss me, too?" Ali hesitantly asked.

Instantly, Zeke let go of her hand to draw her close to him. He brushed his lips across hers lightly. When she eagerly lifted her mouth, Zeke deepened the kiss. This Little girl was as sweet inside as her disposition. When he lifted his head, Zeke stared at her. He loved the faint blush coloring her cheeks. She was absolutely endearing. Unable to resist, he brushed a strand of hair back from her cheek.

He enjoyed that she requested what she wanted. That would be important for a relationship between three people. Zeke had tightened his grip on Ace's hand during their kiss when the younger man had tried to pull away. Now he used their connection to pull Ace back in close. He wrapped his arms around both of their waists and hugged them tightly.

"It is important as we get to know each other that you ask me any questions you wish and tell me anything I need to know. Will you promise me you'll follow those guidelines?" Zeke asked with a serious tone. When they both nodded, he added, "Then, let's get to know each other better. I'll go get towels. When I return, I will ask someone to tell me about your relationship and someone to tell me how you discovered you were Littles. You decide while I'm gone who will answer which question."

Ali looked at Ace. "Can I tell him about Littles? And you can tell him about our relationship?"

Nodding, Ace agreed. Still holding Ali's hand, he looked at her with wide blue eyes. "Do you think it can be that easy? What if he's just playing us?"

"Then, we'll figure it out. We'll never find our Daddy if we don't take a few risks," she answered.

"Here we go. Catch this one, Ace. Stretch that over the blue chair. And Ali, this one's yours. Put that one on the green chair. I'll sit on the couch." Zeke threw the towels as he talked, holding on to one for himself. When Ali didn't move, Zeke looked at her and asked, "Angel, is there somewhere else you'd rather sit."

Shifting from one foot to another, Ali swallowed before gathering her bravery to ask, "Can I sit on the couch with you?" She didn't want to push herself on him, but she'd feel better sitting close.

"Of course," Zeke said, walking forward to wrap his arms around her in a brief hug. "Come on. Let's get our towels arranged so we can sit down and talk."

Three minutes later, they all sat. Ali sat as close to Zeke as she dared. It had delighted her when Zeke patted the cushion next to his towel in a silent invitation to move to the center of the couch. Ace shifted the blue chair over, so they were all clustered together.

As they settled in, Ali blurted, "I get to tell you about Littles." When

Zeke nodded, she rushed ahead. "I like to read a lot. Not the boring stuff that they make you read for school; I like to read about people who fall in love and find their happily ever after. Sometimes, I find books at work when I'm cleaning up. One day, a nice lady was sitting at the end of the bar. She was all alone, so she was reading as she ate lunch. The book must have fallen out of her bag as she got up. I found it wedged by the side of the bar."

Ali paused and looked to Ace for reassurance. When he gave her a thumbs-up, she continued. "I didn't find it until several hours after she left. She's a lady who lives here in town. Her husband is the head of the county police. I planned to keep the book just so I can return it the next time she came in, but the picture on the front made me want to read it. I couldn't get it back to her until the next day, so I decided it wouldn't hurt anything for me to take it home. You know… and bring it back the next day."

When Ali stopped again, Zeke seemed to know that she needed reassurance. He scooped her up in his arms and sat her on his lap. Ali squirmed a bit to make herself comfortable. Then, when she'd settled into place, she continued. "Thanks. The book was about someone just like me. It described all her feelings. I felt as if the author was writing the story about me. The heroine was a Little, and she lived with her Daddy and Mommy."

"Do you think about having a Daddy and Mommy?" Zeke probed.

"No," she admitted. "I skipped all the Mommy parts. They didn't interest me at all. But I loved the parts about her relationship with him. You know, with her Daddy?"

"What did you like best?"

"He loved her so much. She was so lucky to have him take care of her—completely. Ace and I have been together forever. Neither one of us enjoys taking care of grown-up stuff. He asked me what I was reading. I had to tell him about my fantasies. We don't keep anything from each other. I almost fell out of bed in shock when he admitted that he had the same desires."

Ace tried to explain his part. "Ali and I have shared an apartment since we graduated from high school. We've experimented with other people individually, but I've loved her since the first day we met. She knows I'm drawn to men. It doesn't bother her."

"You've never had sex with a man?" Zeke asked softly.

"I've never even kissed a man before today," the young man admitted. "It was pretty awesome." Ace grinned at him in delight.

"I'm glad you enjoyed our kiss. I thought it was special as well. I just didn't know how special." Zeke reached a hand out to Ace. When he meshed his fingers with Zeke's, the older man asked, "What do you think about sharing Ali with another man? Will you be able to watch her with someone else?"

Ace's eyes lit with desire. "That would be so hot. It wouldn't bother me because she wants to be with her Daddy and me." Ace looked down at the floor for a few seconds and added, "I felt bad for a while. I wished I could be a Daddy for her, but I'm just not wired that way."

"Oh, no! Ace, I wouldn't ever want you to pretend to be anything that you're not! That would never work!" Ali leaned forward toward Ace and waggled her fingers to motion him toward her. When he cooperated, she squeezed him in a tight hug. Then, she sat back against Zeke's chest.

"Ali, I need to ask you the same question. Are you sure that you could watch a man make love to Ace?" Zeke asked. He leaned sideways away from her to watch her face.

"I have seen men have sex. You know, like on the internet? I agree with Ace. Seeing him with someone else would be hot. It would be bonfire hot if he was with someone that cared about both of us." Ali's face fell slightly as she hesitated. Curling against Zeke's chest, she hid her face in his soft T-shirt.

Stroking her back to reassure her, Zeke softly reassured her, "You can tell me anything, Little girl. That's how it should be between Littles and their Daddies. Can you talk to me?"

Several seconds ticked by. Ace leaned forward a little more to rub his hand over her slender thigh. Neither man rushed her. Zeke would give her a bit to decide whether she was comfortable sharing whatever troubled her.

Words tumbled from Ali's mouth, "I think the worst thing would be if someone loved Ace more than me or vice versa. Is it possible for a Daddy to love each of us equally?"

"Yes," Zeke said, succinctly.

"That's it? It's that easy?" she asked, meeting his gaze before looking over to check in with Ace.

"It is that easy. There may be times if you get in trouble and Ace has not." He paused as they both burst out laughing. Shaking his head, Zeke continued. "As unlikely as you both seem to think that would be—you may believe that I love him more. That would be untrue. I couldn't call myself a Daddy to more than one Little without being sure that I could deeply care for two people at the same time."

The worry on Ali's face dissipated. Zeke leaned in to kiss her softly. "I want you to promise me if you ever feel that I do not cherish each of you separately as well as together that you will talk to me. A Daddy sometimes needs help to be the best Daddy he can be."

"Do we get to spank you?" Ace asked, waggling his eyebrows comically.

"No." Zeke looked back and forth between the two Littles. "You've obviously thought of some punishments that Daddies might decide to use. We'll talk about those more later. I'd also like you to think about the rewards that mean the most to you. Good behavior should be acknowledged, just as bad behavior should be."

Ace's stomach roared ferociously, and he clapped his hand over his abdomen. When both Ali's and Zeke's echoed that sound, they looked at each other before bursting into laughter.

"Does everyone likes pizza? I think you can have that delivered here," Zeke asked, looking for confirmation from the two natives.

"Pietro's is the best," Ali shared.

Zeke pulled up the menu on his phone. Scrolling through the listings quickly, he asked, "What's your favorite?"

"I like cheese, but Ali likes everything on her pizza. We usually get one half-and-half," Ace explained.

"Got it." Zeke phoned the restaurant to place in an order for two large pizzas, one a deluxe cheese, and the other, a combination. After giving them his address, Zeke hung up. "I'm getting scaly from all the salt. Let's get cleaned up before the pizza gets here. If you don't mind wearing some borrowed clothes, I'll be glad to loan you something to wear."

When they both eagerly agreed, Zeke let them back in his room. "There are two showers, one in the hall bathroom, and the other in this master bathroom." He opened a drawer and pulled out two T-shirts and a pair of shorts. "All of this will be too big, but it's clean. I'd like to help each of you into the shower. Will you let me do that?"

For the first time, Ace looked shy. He nodded, looking down at his feet. Zeke approached and wrapped his arms around the fit young man. "There's no rush."

"I want you to help me. I'm just afraid I'll do something wrong. My dick's already hard," Ace admitted, shifting his hands over his pelvis.

"There aren't any wrongs here, wild boy. However your body reacts and however you feel is right. You can't hide from your Daddy. That I will not allow." Calmly, Zeke moved Ace's hands to his sides. When he resisted, Zeke whispered to him privately, "I'm older with more muscles, but you're younger with more energy. This is where we find out if you really want a Daddy or not. Will you submit to my care?"

Ace raised his gaze to meet Zeke's green eyes. His hands moved quickly to his sides and flattened against his thighs. "I want this—as much as I need Ali in my life."

"I think I can work with that," Zeke answered. His tone was serious, but he felt his lips curve in a smile at the earnest response. Before Ace could worry more, Zeke lifted the young man's T-shirt over his head and hooked his index fingers into Ace's light blue swim trunks. Skillfully easing them over his erection, Zeke drew them down to his knees and let them go.

When they puddled at his feet, Zeke instructed, "Step out, Little boy." Zeke allowed his eyes to scan his nude body. Raising his gaze to meet Ace's, he permitted him to see the desire reflected in his eyes.

"You are handsome, wild boy. Let me start the water for you," Zeke said, raising a hand to cup Ace's jaw. Zeke brushed his thumb over his full lips before stepping forward to kiss him lightly. He wrapped an arm around Ace's waist and guided him into the bathroom. After adjusting the water, he ushered him into the shower.

Before closing the door, Zeke promised, "Next time, I'll join you." A flash of desire flared in the Little's brown eyes. Zeke maintained eye contact until the clouded glass separated them.

Ali stood precisely where he had left her. Her hand pressed against her mouth after hungrily watching the men. Picking up the large T-shirt that would fit her like a dress, Zeke wrapped an arm around her waist and guided her to the hall bathroom. Ushering her in front of him, he dropped the shirt on the vanity before turning to Ali. "All right, angel Little. Let's get this sandy suit off of you so you can get clean as well. Use whatever you'd like. There are shampoo, conditioner, and bath soap all on the ledge inside."

"Okay," she answered and reached behind her neck to begin untying her bathing suit.

Zeke moved close to run his hands over her forearms, halting her fingers. "That's Daddy's job. Will you let me undress you?" When she nodded and lowered her hands, Zeke took over and unfastened the top string of her bikini, allowing it to flip down. His eyes caressed her beautiful breasts as he stroked down her spine to find the bottom strap. Releasing it, he allowed the scraps of material to drop to the ground. Zeke traced a path over her torso's sensitive skin to hook his fingers in the top of her bikini bottoms. Quickly, they too lay on the floor.

Just as he had with Ace, Zeke allowed his gaze to run over her sweet body. Her small breasts would fit perfectly in his hands. Her body was lean and muscular. Obviously, Ali worked and played hard. Lifting a hand to brush through her tousled hair, he met her blue eyes and held her gaze for several long seconds before leaning in to touch her pink lips with his.

As the kiss ended, Zeke whispered from inches away, "What a beautiful Little girl. I am a very lucky Daddy. Come get in the shower." Her answering smile was radiant. Taking a step back, he drew her to the shower doors. Once again, he turned on the water and helped his Little step inside. "Take your time, Little one."

CHAPTER 4

Picking up the sandy bikini, Zeke stopped just outside the bathroom door to adjust his rigid erection. Retracing his steps into the master bedroom, he picked up Ace's things. The sound of each shower running was a pure temptation.

As he walked to the washing machine, Zeke pulled his sun shirt over his head with one hand. Three of them could have all fit in the large shower where Ace now stood. Shaking his head, he lectured himself to go slow. The Littles needed to know him better. Would the time he had allotted for his vacation be long enough for the three of them to discover if this relationship could be what they'd all been looking to find?

"Hell! I don't even know if they are willing to move to SANCTUM." Zeke cursed aloud as he dropped the clothes into the washer. Dashing into the living room, he grabbed the towels and threw them in the washer as well. After adding soap, Zeke shucked off his own swim trunks to add to the machine. With the press of a button, he started the cycle.

His hand automatically wrapped around his erection as he thought of Ace and Ali. They were young. He hadn't seen their age for a long time. "Maybe I'm too old for them."

"You're not too old," a masculine voice disagreed.

"Come on, Daddy. We're all showering together," Ali announced.

Zeke looked up to see the two Littles wet, but wrapped in towels. Ali approached and held out a hand. Automatically, he lifted his hand from his penis to take hers. As she tugged him down the hallway, Ace followed. His hands wrapped around Zeke's shoulders, urging him on when he paused in the hallway. "You got this all worked out, do you?"

One of Ace's hands rose from Zeke's shoulders. The younger man drew a damp line down Zeke's back. "Looks like you're just as sandy as we are."

When they got into the master bathroom, Ali and Ace dropped their towels before continuing the pushing and pulling process of getting Zeke into the shower. As Ace turned the water back on, Zeke ducked his head under the showerhead to give himself a second to regain control. Two sets of hands immediately smoothed soap over his body.

Dashing the water out of his eyes, Zeke focused on the scene before him. The slippery soap felt good on his salt-roughened skin. He allowed Ace and Ali to touch him. When their hands closed around his erection, Zeke permitted each of them to stroke him once from root to tip before lifting their hands from his body.

"Good Littles always get to come first," Zeke informed them as he lifted their hands from his shaft. "Besides, it's my turn. Who's first?"

Ali wiggled in front of Ace, who stepped back good-naturedly. "Me! It's my turn!"

Zeke poured some liquid bath soap onto his hands. When Ace held his hand out for the bottle, Zeke shook his head. "Only Daddy gets to wash his Littles this time." Ace opened his mouth to protest. Then, obviously trying to follow directions, he stepped back to the corner of the shower. There alone, he leaned against the wall and sulked.

Ignoring his Little boy's attitude, Zeke spread the lather over Ali's shoulders and arms. When he finished with her fingers, he turned his attention to her torso. Stroking across her collarbones, Zeke watched her chest lift in anticipation as she took a quick breath. He did not make her wait long. His fingers stroked along the sides of each small breast before circling to smooth the slick suds over her skin. His thumbs brushed over her tightly clenched nipples, making her gasp sharply.

My Little girl is very sensitive. He repeated the caress several times until her eyelids dropped slightly. Stroking down her rib cage and abdomen, Zeke paused just above the mound between her thighs. Allowing the tension to build slightly, he stepped forward to wrap his left arm around Ali's waist. His lips met hers softly as his fingers slipped through the sparse hair to trace the seam of her outer labia.

Ali stepped wider, and Zeke rewarded her nonverbal request for him to touch more intimately. His hand cupped her most private area and squeezed. He could feel her heat and savored her arousal. Dipping his fingers into her wetness, Zeke deepened his kiss, distracting her as he sought her sensitive spots. When she gasped into his mouth, Zeke lifted his mouth from hers.

"Daddy?" she asked. Her hands clutched his body for stability as Zeke explored her. When he stepped back to allow the water to rinse away the suds, she protested, "No!"

"Don't want the soap to sting," he explained. When she protested, he placed one finger across her lips. "Daddy's in charge. Turn around." He waited for her to follow directions. After several seconds, she rotated and earned his praise. "Good girl!"

Zeke quickly cleaned her back and spread the soap over her small buttocks. Again tracing the division, Zeke instructed, "Put your hands on the tile. Daddy will wash your bottom." Aware that Ace watched closely, he traced a finger over that small, clenched opening between her cheeks. "Daddy will have to prepare you to accept him here also," he shared as his finger pressed inward. Both Littles breathed in sharply, Ali in reaction to the sting of the soap and Ace in anticipation.

Removing the tip of his finger from her tight bottom, Zeke once again turned her to allow the water to rinse the suds from her body. With her back against the cascade of water, Zeke walked around to kneel in front of her. He stroked a hand down Ali's thigh as he moved into position. Zeke quickly washed the salt and sand from her legs before instructing her to turn in a slow circle to rinse away all the soap and grime.

He steadied her with a hand on her sides at hip level. Leaning forward, he traced that seam once again, but this time with his tongue. Ali's sweet flavor spread across his taste buds. Her breath came faster, and she shifted eagerly to spread her legs. From the corner of his eye, Zeke saw Ace move forward slightly so he could watch. When the Little boy's hand gripped his penis, Zeke lifted his face from Ali's body to order, "Hands behind your back, wild boy."

While Zeke waited to see if he would obey, Ali begged, "Ace! Please! Do as he asks!" Zeke was pleased when Ace slowly lifted his hands before gripping them behind his back. "Good job, Little boy."

His mouth pressed back into Ali's sweet juices. Using his fingers to caress her, Zeke drove Ali into a fast, massive orgasm. He gentled his caresses and lifted his mouth from her body. Smoothly, he rose to his feet and pulled her against his hard body. Pressing his lips once again to hers, Zeke allowed her to taste her own flavor that filled his mouth. Her groan went straight to his erection and drew a low moan from the man who watched.

When she had recovered and could stand steadily, Zeke whispered, "Go trade places with Ace. Give him a kiss for having been so patient to allow you to go first."

Ali wobbled to Ace's side. His arms escaped from their clutched position behind him. One hand wrapped around the back of her head to pull her lips to his. Ali clung to his body for stability as his pent-up passion flowed over her. With a whimper, Ali ripped her mouth from his and urged Ace toward Zeke. She leaned against the tiled wall for support as she turned to watch.

Stalking forward, Ace pressed himself against Zeke. When he tried to control the kiss, Zeke stepped backward. "You are not in charge with Daddy," he sternly corrected Ace. "Put your hands behind your back."

Ace stared at him in disbelief. Again, he reached out for Zeke, but the older man backed away. "I can't touch you?" Ace demanded.

"When you understand how to be truly Little, I will give you permission. For now, no." Zeke steadily held his gaze until Ace slowly moved his hands behind his back. Zeke could see the young man's biceps bulging as he tried to follow directions and fought himself from his natural urge to touch. "Good Little boys earn rewards. Thank you, Ace."

Taking his time, Zeke coated his hands with liquid soap. When he was ready, he stepped forward to stroke the slippery mixture over Ace's shoulders and arms. He could feel the tiny quivers of the young man's muscles as he touched Ace's toned body. Zeke slowly and deliberately washed his chest and abdomen. His pelvis pushed forward in the silent plea for him to lavish attention on Ace's rigid shaft.

"Turn around," Zeke instructed. He did not allow any emotion to show in his eyes as Ace looked at him in disbelief. "Turn around. Put your hands on the tile and lean forward."

Whirling, Ace followed his instructions and assumed the position required. Again, Zeke deliberately moved as he cleaned the salt and sand from the young man's back. Skipping his tight buttocks, Zeke knelt behind Ace to wash his legs. He allowed his fingers to brush his sac as he finished with attention to Ace's inner thighs.

A low moan echoed against the tile as Ace dropped his forehead to the cool surface. Rising to his feet, Zeke focused on those tight buns displayed before him. At his touch, Ace pressed his bottom toward the caresses in a silent invitation. Zeke's fingers traced the crevice, dipping inside to press against the small hidden opening. Ace bucked back toward that exploring hand. When Zeke's finger pressed inward, Ace's head arched backward.

Only then did Zeke reach around his body. Wrapping his fingers around Ace's throbbing erection, Zeke stroked up and down his shaft. A low moan echoed once again. On his next stroke downward, Zeke brushed over Ace's heavy sac and tugged gently. He repeated this caress in an unrecognizable pattern—a rough pull upward followed by a downward stroke with that infrequent teasing tug.

When Zeke knew Ace had focused on his pelvis, his teasing finger at the Little's anus pressed deep. Ace froze in place for several seconds. His mind appeared to be trying to process all the sensations lavished on his body. With a roar, Ace thrust desperately into Zeke's grasp. His body erupted.

Zeke gentled his touch. Removing that invading finger, he turned Ace to face him and pulled him into the tight embrace. The Little wrapped his arms around Zeke and clung to him. Zeke took Ace's lips in a fiercely rewarding kiss. When he released the back of Ace's head, the Little moved to nestle against him. Zeke whispered reassurances and pressed kisses to his skin.

As Ace's breath recovered, Zeke held out one arm in a silent invitation for Ali to join them. With a soft cry, she bolted into his arms. Zeke squeezed the two Littles against his body. They felt so good in his arms. *Please let them decide they belong with me.* He'd just confirmed that they were his.

He held them close, unwilling to be separated from his Littles, until the hot water began to cool. Immediately, Zeke turned Ace into the stream of water, making sure he had rinsed all the suds from his body. Then turning off the shower, Zeke wrapped each Little in a towel and helped them step out of the shower. When they were safely out of the spray of rapidly chilling water, he closed the shower door and quickly cleaned himself. To his delight, his Littles followed his guidance to step out of the shower without protest. They were learning how to be Little.

CHAPTER 5

Zeke stepped out of the shower and heard the doorbell ring. He stopped to press a kiss against both Ali and Zeke's foreheads. "Dry off and get dressed. The pizza is here." He wrapped a towel around his dripping body and strode to the door.

He grabbed his wallet on the way to the door. Opening it, he found a young woman holding two large boxes. The aroma of hot Italian pizza confirmed that his Littles knew which was the best place for delivery. He watched the delivery driver's eyes widen before they traced over his exposed body. Reaching the towel, her gaze focused on the erection that the icy water hadn't erased.

Clearing his throat, Zeke held out a healthy tip. Her cheeks flushed a delightful pink. A whisper of movement behind him drew her attention. Zeke felt the terry cloth brush against his back as Ali leaned around him. She appeared to reveal her presence deliberately and hint at intimacy by her obvious nudity under the towel.

"Hi, Jamie! Thanks for bringing the pizza. Don't forget your tip."

Jolted from her perusal, Jamie blushed again before relinquishing the boxes and accepting the money. Zeke saw her glance over her shoulder several times as he closed the door.

"You may not be the angel Little that I first thought," he laughed. Just at that moment, Ace walked down the hallway dressed in the slightly oversized clothing that Zeke had loaned him. "On second thought, maybe I got the two of you mixed up and Ace is my Little angel."

A sniff drew his attention back to Ali. Her blue eyes welled with tears. "Are you claiming us?"

"Oh, Little girl. I think the more important question is whether I'm the right Daddy for you and whether your feelings are strong enough to help you decide to follow me to SANCTUM." Zeke held up a hand to stop her from answering. "This can't be a rash decision. I want my Littles forever."

Zeke held the pizza boxes to the side and stepped forward to draw her against him. "I hope that SANCTUM will soon have two new Littles." He kissed her tenderly before stepping away.

"Ace, I'm going to trust you not to eat both pizzas while we throw on some clothes. Explore the kitchen a bit and find the plates." When Ace took the boxes from him, the Little also leaned in for his kiss, pleasing Zeke. He made a mental note that he would need to make sure that each Little received equal attention.

A short time later, everyone gathered around the kitchen table, Ace tried to relax. It wasn't that Zeke made him nervous. He was afraid to do something that would ruin everything for not only him, but Ali. He didn't think his restlessness was apparent to anyone, but Zeke scooted his chair closer to lay his hand on top of Ace's. The older man squeezed his fingers slightly as he continued his story about learning to surf.

"No way! When you finally got up, your first thought was that there were sharks underneath you?" Ali laughed. "How quickly did you fall off?"

"I didn't. I rode the board all the way into shore," Zeke laughed. "I amazed the pros teaching us. When they told me to head back out, there were all these cute girls around. I couldn't admit that I was scared, so I paddled back out. When nothing ate me that day, I was hooked. Ace, how old were you when you started surfing?"

Ace rushed to answer, "I was ten. My mom wouldn't let me try until I was as tall as the surfer statue at the rental shack on the beach. I'm glad I didn't think about sharks."

"Oooh! It was so cute! I remember seeing you standing next to the statue each week, checking to see if you got tall enough yet. When Ace knew how, he shared his board to teach me." Ali snagged another piece of the combo pizza. "Mmm! This is so good. Pietro's is the best. I think I could eat pizza every day."

"I am impressed. This pizza is delicious. I don't know which one is better. The plain cheese is amazing with all the fresh cheeses and that sauce! I think the combo pizza weighs a ton. It has everything on it," Zeke commented as he had another piece of that pizza as well.

"Thank you very much! Ali always makes fun of me because I love the cheese pizza. It doesn't need anything else." Ace took a big bite and chewed. He studied Zeke as he talked to Ali. The older man was handsome. A few silver threads glistened in his brown hair. He wondered how rude it was to ask his age. Swallowing, he decided to go for it.

When there was a lull in the conversation, he asked, "Zeke, how old are you?"

Ali protested, as Zeke laughed, "Ace!" She frowned at him and tried to signal him with their eyes to stop. They'd been together long enough that Ace could read her subtle facial expressions and silent messages.

"I'm not trying to be rude. I was just curious."

"You can ask me anything, Little boy. I'm happy you want to know more about me. I'm forty-two. I married right out of high school, and it lasted two years. We both knew we made a mistake almost immediately. Brenda had been such a wonderful friend that I didn't want to hurt her by asking for a divorce. Turns out, she was hesitating for the same reason."

"Do you have any kids?" Ali asked, dropping her pizza down to her plate.

"No."

"I'm the baby in the group," Ace joked and then realized that his usual joke had a different meaning in this company. "You know, the youngest person. Not the baby. I am twenty-five."

"And according to Ace, I'm ancient at twenty-six." Ali shot a meaningful glance at Ace. "Maybe I should get you a pacifier next year for your birthday?"

"Wanting the pacifier is not a shameful thing, Ali. Many Littles enjoy adult-sized versions of many products made for babies," Zeke interrupted her teasing.

"I was just being silly." Her face fell, and the corners of her mouth trembled slightly.

"I know you're not trying to be mean, Ali. You don't have a malicious bone in your body." Ace took a big breath and let it out in a shaky gust of air. His eyes fixed on the wooden table. He forced the truth out of his mouth. Something that he had never even admitted to Ali. "I think I'm supposed to be really Little. You know, in the books we've read, Littles are all different ages. I guess they call them Middles when they're older." His voice trailed off as he lost his courage. Ace focused on the table, scared to see their reaction. After a scrape of the chair, a warm, muscular arm wrapped around him. Ali's small hand covered his to squeeze it reassuringly.

"It's important for Littles to be the age that's best for them. I think it would be best to experiment a bit to find what age fits each of you. I would be astonished if you are both the same Little age. I'll have some supplies overnighted to me and we'll explore what is best," Zeke suggested. "First on my list will be bottles and pacifiers."

Ace dared to meet Zeke's eyes. His breath sighed from his mouth in a gust of relief. The older man's expression was kind, caring, and affectionate. Leaning in, Ace pressed his lips softly against Zeke's. The arm around his shoulders stroked his back.

Zeke reached a hand across the table to Ali. Her fingers closed on it immediately. Ace watched as she struggled to say something important. He knew she'd talk when she was ready. For several minutes, they sat quietly. The silence was comfortable and reassuring. Ali could take the time she needed.

"I dream of having a Daddy who cares for me in different ways. If I don't feel well … like I'm tired or sick, my dream Daddy would take care of me, too, with those items. But if I'm happy and energetic, I'd want to be a big girl with a purple sippy cup decorated with unicorns or baby animals." Ali clapped her free hand over her mouth to stop more details from tumbling from her lips.

Ace watched the smile that widened on Zeke's face as she talked. He winked at Ali as her cheeks blushed pink. He knew she'd pretended to be bigger than she needed to be.

"I think I can arrange all of that." Zeke's answer was simple and accepting.

"Really?" Ali squeaked.

"Any tummies need more pizza?" Zeke asked, looking at the last two pieces remaining in the box. He laughed when both Littles sat up straight and dropped any hands they held to claim another slice.

Zeke disposed of the cardboard in the recycling bin. Glancing at the clock, he smiled. It was time for his Littles to start their new lives. They wouldn't know if they were meant for this lifestyle unless they tried it. Returning to the table, he chatted with Ali and Ace, getting to know them better.

"So, you both work as bartenders. Is that what you have always wanted to do?"

Shaking her head, Ali swallowed the bite in her mouth before answering. "I thought I wanted to be a nurse. It turns out there's a lot of icky stuff with being a nurse that I didn't like. I started on my certified nurse's aide classes and dropped out after three weeks. It just wasn't for me."

"You should have seen her! She came home every night and washed her hands like four hundred times. Ali really likes people, but she's awful in an emergency. I tried to warn her," Ace added with a laugh.

"Oh, yeah! Like your attempt to learn diesel repair. You walked around with a perpetual hard-on due to all the men's butts stretched over car engines," Ali replied.

"None of that, now," Zeke sternly corrected. "When we're together, we're a family that supports each other. Lots of people try different careers and decide that it's not right for them. Admitting that you made a mistake is much better than stubbornly sticking to what you thought you might like but discover you hate. There are a lot of unhappy people out there in jobs they detest. Better to make a change now."

"Sorry, Ali…"

"No, you were right. I never thought my hands would be clean again. I'm sorry, too. You can't help how your body reacts."

As they smiled at each other across the table, Zeke felt something click in place deep inside him. He could see these two and himself creating a family. Before he jumped too far ahead, Zeke tried to rein in his thoughts. He distracted himself by asking, "Everyone finished with dinner?"

When both Littles chimed in with a yes, Zeke announced, "It's bedtime!"

"Bedtime? It's only seven. I don't go to bed until at least eleven or midnight," Ace protested. Ali agreed with him immediately.

"Littles go to bed much earlier than that. They need lots of sleep to feel their best."

Ali's expression shifted from protest to sadness. "Are you trying to get rid of us?"

Zeke crossed the dining area to her chair. Tugging her up, he sat down in her place before pulling her onto his lap. With her cuddled in his arms, he answered, "Never! I would keep you here forever, but I know this has been an emotionally packed day for us. Be honest. Are you tired?"

Starting to shake her head, Ali hesitated before nodding. "But I don't want to leave."

"Me, neither," Ace chimed in.

"That's a good thing. We should enjoy spending time together. I can't wait to learn more about you both, but sleep is important. Let's make a plan for tomorrow. When do you work?"

"We both work the long shift tomorrow. Lunch and dinner," Ace clarified.

"And on the following day?"

"We just work at dinner. Our shift starts at four," Ali reported.

"How about if I come to eat at the bar tomorrow? That way we'll see each other. I know you'll be busy working. I don't want you to get in trouble for chatting with me too much," Zeke warned.

"Sit at my end of the bar this time," Ace urged after nodding his agreement.

"Deal," Zeke agreed. "Then the next day, we'll spend the morning together. Would you like to leave your surfboards here? I'll hold them hostage until you come back," he joked, trying to cheer up the Littles.

"Yes!" Ali agreed immediately. "Are you really going to make us leave?"

"I'm sending you home so you can go to sleep to be ready to work that long shift tomorrow. Being a Daddy requires that I do what's best for you, regardless that I'd love for you to stay." Squeezing his arms around the Little girl one last time, Zeke boosted her up to stand.

He took her hand before taking Ace's. "How did you get to the beach?"

"We walked," Ace whispered.

"Let me grab my keys, and I'll drive you home."

"Our apartment is kind of a mess," Ali admitted.

"You'll invite me in a different day. Tonight, I want you to brush your teeth, kiss each other good night, and jump in bed. No shenanigans."

"Do shenanigans mean sex?" Ace asked with a grin.

"Yes, and no touching yourself either."

"You're taking away all our fun," Ace joked.

"No. I'm just making sure we share our intimate time from now on."

Ali and Ace were quiet for a moment before Ali decided, "That makes it more special."

"Definitely," Zeke agreed before pulling them in for one last hug. He forced himself to corral them toward the door. Picking up his keys, he took one more look around the house that now seemed more like a home.

CHAPTER 6

Returning home to a quiet house, Zeke marveled at the difference two Littles could make. He busied himself by taking the bathing suits out of the washer to air-dry and putting the towels in the dryer. Silence surrounded him like never before.

He circled the house, making sure he'd locked everything for the night before heading to the master bedroom. While brushing his teeth, he hoped that Ace and Ali were already in bed and drifting off to sleep. Zeke finished his routine and disrobed. The crisp sheets were cold as he slid between them.

Turning on the TV to check the news, Zeke allowed his mind to wander. He replayed the day's events, trying to determine the exact moment he'd decided that Ali and Ace were his. He'd talked to other Mommies and Daddies who had shared how quickly they'd known that a Little was meant to be theirs. Inside, he had scoffed that anyone could know something that important so fast. He now knew how wrong he'd been.

The buzz of his phone interrupted his thoughts. Picking it up, he saw the notification. A second appeared a breath later. Opening up his messages, Zeke saw two enchanting images. The first featured Ace reclined on the fluffy pillow holding a stuffed lion in his arms.

Eagerly, he tapped on the second. Ali blew a kiss to him from her bed in a short video.

From her angle, Zeke could see that his two Littles shared a bedroom, narrow twin beds pressed against opposite walls. Pulling up his phone, he returned each message with an image of him in bed as well. He followed by wishing them sweet dreams and a warning to turn off their phones and go to sleep.

The streaming sunlight that invaded their bedroom the next morning woke him. Checking the clock on the nightstand, Ace was astonished to see that he'd slept eleven hours. "Ali! Ali, wake up!"

"What time is it?" she mumbled, still half-asleep.

"It's eight o'clock!"

"Eight o'clock? We slept forever." Stumbling out of bed, Ali crossed the carpet between them and crawled into bed with Ace. She snuggled against him.

"It took me a while to get to sleep," he confessed. "I kept thinking about our day and about Zeke. Do you think he could really be our Daddy?"

"I think so. It kind of boggles my mind. I've been on the lookout for a Daddy since I first read that book. When we didn't find anybody, I'd started to believe that maybe they didn't exist," Ali confessed.

"Me, too." Ace turned on his side to loop an arm around her waist. Giving her a tight squeeze, he pressed a light kiss to her lips. "Do you think it was all a dream?"

Ali turned and grabbed his cell phone from the nightstand. "Silly! Double-check that his picture is there." She looked on as Ace unlocked his phone and clicked on the messages. They both grinned at each other upon seeing Zeke's picture. Exchanging a celebratory hug, Ali said, "It actually happened."

"I really like him. Do you think he likes us?"

"He's incredible. I do think he likes us," Ali tried to reassure them both.

"The test will be if he comes to the bar today. I'll feel a lot better when I see him walk in."

"I wish we didn't work all day today." Ali's lower lip stuck out slightly. All she wanted to do was spend the day with the enchanting man that had so recently come into their lives.

Playfully, Ace leaned in to nip at her pouting lip, setting off a wrestling session. Ali rolled on top of him to pin him to the mattress. She froze in place at the feel of his morning erection pressed solidly against her pink panties. Zeke's words flooded back into her brain. "Daddy said no," she reminded Ace when he lifted his pelvis to press against her warmth.

Groaning, Ace turned to the side to dump the temptation off his body. "You called him Daddy," he whispered before dropping one arm over his eyes in frustration.

"It just seemed right." Doubts flooded into her brain. Everything had moved so fast. Was it possible that he was as perfect for them as she thought?

The rustle of bedclothes and a dip in the mattress pulled her out of her worries. She turned her head to see Ace propped up on one elbow, looking down at her. "This is what we dreamed of for a long time. What can it hurt to explore our attraction to him? If it doesn't work, Zeke will leave for SANCTUM without us."

Instantly, something inside Ali broke. Tears streamed down her face. She turned to hide against Ace's broad chest. His arms wrapped around her and squeezed her tightly against his body. "I don't want him to leave us. How can I feel this strongly after this short amount of time?"

Stroking his hand down the length of her spine, Ace shared, "I loved you the first time we met. Anyone who would share her stuffie with a complete stranger deserved my heart. I think it's possible that you can care about someone when you've just met. If it follows our pattern, we'll love him more with each amount of time we spend together. If not, maybe it's not a genuine relationship."

Ali leaned back to meet his deep brown eyes. "How did you get so smart?"

"Innate genius," he declared before pushing her out of his bed.

Laughing hard, Ali scrambled to her feet. "The first one out of bed gets to use the bathroom first!"

As the bathroom door closed, she heard, "I'm coming in after ten minutes—ready or not!" Laughing, she got ready for the day. There was no way to solve the dilemma of Zeke. She just had to see what happened. *Too bad crystal balls don't really exist.*

CHAPTER 7

Ace tried not to watch the clock. The lunch crowd had streamed in when the doors opened. An influx of locals and tourists kept the seats filled. He usually loved working for the popular restaurant. The hopping busyness made the time speed past each day. Each time his section at the bar filled, Ace hoped Zeke would not appear and have to sit elsewhere.

"He's not here yet," Ali worried about one o'clock.

"He'll be here," Ace reassured her with more confidence than he really felt. The lunch crowd was thinning out when a familiar figure caught his eye. He elbowed Ali before waving.

As Zeke settled into a barstool, the two young bartenders hovered close. "Hey, you two!" The heat in his eyes gave Ace the impression that Zeke wished he could greet them more intimately.

"Ali was concerned. She thought you weren't coming," Ace admitted, throwing his partner in crime under the bus.

"Ace!" Ali protested, giving him a look of death.

Zeke laughed at the exchange before apologizing, "I'm sorry I worried you, Ali. You too, Ace. I thought if I came in for a late lunch, maybe you'd have more time to chat. I should have texted you to tell you about my plans. Will you forgive me?"

Both Littles nodded. That made perfect sense to Ace. Changing the topic, Ace asked, "Are you hungry?"

"I could eat a hippopotamus. What do you suggest?"

"Ali loves the fish and chips, as you know. They're good," Ace allowed before adding, "My favorite is the seafood platter. It's a lot of food. But if you're hungry, it's the way to go."

"Bring it on," Zeke said with dancing eyes.

"Can I choose something for you to drink, too?"

"Make it something nonalcoholic. I'm going to drive around this afternoon while you all are at work. I've got some things to pick up."

"I can help you with directions," Ace offered.

"Thank you. I got my GPS. It'll take me everywhere I need to go. But I'll take you up on that when I have some things to do in town."

"I'll put in your order and get you something to drink." Ace scurried off to complete his tasks. It wasn't until he was at the computer typing in Zeke's order when he processed the older man's words. He was leaving town! Quickly, he pressed Enter and sent the order to the kitchen before returning to Zeke's side.

"You're coming back, aren't you?" Ace asked, leaning on the bar to get a little closer to this dynamic man.

"Definitely. I have the house for two weeks. The three of us will talk a lot before that time is up," he promised. Zeke reached across the bar to run his hand from Ace's shoulder to rest on his forearm. "I won't disappear. Not now."

Ace felt his shoulders settle back down into place as the tension that had built so quickly dissipated. "Okay. Let me get you something to drink." Grabbing a shaker, Ace poured together a mixture of juices with a dash of this and that. He could feel Zeke's eyes on him as he demonstrated his flashy bartending moves. Ace wanted to impress his Daddy.

Mentally he crossed his fingers, hoping that Zeke would love this refreshing drink. He had created it himself for a customer who was jaded with all the typical tropical beverages. That customer had raved about it and had even written a review on the restaurant's website. The manager had been so impressed that he made Ace the employee of the month.

"Oh! You're making Daddy a Tropical Acealanche!" Ali clapped her hands in delight. "I love those!" Ali had named it for Ace combining his name and avalanche. The drink made with three kinds of alcohol was illegal—like being swept away by an avalanche. "I love the virgin version!" Her mouth got tangled up as she tried to say those last two words.

"Try saying that three times fast," Zeke laughed.

With a flourish, Ace poured the mixture into a tall glass filled with crushed ice. He placed it in front of Zeke and bowed slightly. "Your drink, sir." He threw a towel over his forearm as if he worked in a five-star restaurant.

As Zeke took the first sip, the patron sitting to his left commented, "That looks good. Can you make me one, or are they only for special guests?"

"This is delicious, Ace. You should definitely try this," Zeke remarked to the man one stool over.

Ace quickly concocted another but added alcohol as the patron desired. He tried to be very professional, but inside he wanted to have his Daddy all to himself. He didn't want the other man involved in their conversation. To his relief, the hostess called the other man's name almost as soon as he had his first sip. The customer left the two of them alone as he followed the young woman to the available table.

Leaning on the bar, Ace looked over to check how Ali was doing. They worked together. If she was swamped, he helped her and vice versa. He was glad to see she had several customers, but nothing that she couldn't handle. Ace had a bit of time to talk to Zeke privately. He stared at the rubber mat, edging the top of the bar, and tried to figure out what he should say. When Zeke's hand covered his, he looked up into those green eyes.

"I won't disappear, Ace. That's not the type of person I am, and it's not the relationship I'm looking to establish. I've searched for you and Ali for years," Zeke shared. His eyes held Ace's steadily to reassure him.

"You're here as a visitor for two weeks," Ace pointed out.

"I am," Zeke admitted. "I created my schedule arbitrarily. Originally, I just wanted to hang out at the beach and have a brief break while my house was being finished at SANCTUM. I never dreamed that I'd find my Littles. Now my focus has changed."

"How can you be so sure..." Ace's voice trailed off as a couple sat down at the bar next to Zeke. He smiled ruefully before moving over to greet the couple.

After creating a couple of mouthwatering frozen drinks, Ace ran back to the kitchen to check on Zeke's food. He hefted the large platter and carried it to the bar. "Just as I promised you, the best of everything," he said, placing it in front of the handsome man.

"I think I will take your advice from now on," Zeke declared, looking at the delicacies arranged in front of him. "I don't know where to start."

"Try the deviled crab," Ali suggested as she passed them on the way to the kitchen. "It's my favorite." She hovered for a moment to point out the filled shell in the center of his plate.

"Thank you, Ali," Zeke replied with a smile. He picked up his fork and took the first bite. "Mmm! If the rest is as good, I may just camp out here at the bar." Ali smiled and raced off to put in an order.

"What is that?" the man next to him asked, waving a hand toward the large platter.

"It's the seafood platter. The expert recommended it for me," Zeke answered with a smile as he nodded to Ace.

"Honey, let's split one of those. It looks like it has everything on it," the man suggested to his wife.

Ace passed Ali on his way to the kitchen to put in the couple's order. He gathered her in a quick hug and kissed her cheek. Just the feel of her body against his was reassuring.

"You okay?" she asked, giving him an extra squeeze.

"I want this so bad."

"Me, too," she admitted before racing back to the bar.

When Ace returned to the bar, his eyes automatically checked on Zeke first. When the older man winked at him and gave him a thumbs-up, Ace celebrated with a few dance moves to his Daddy's amusement. As everyone laughed at his antics, Ace checked on his other customers quickly. Without missing a beat, he headed back to talk to the man who intrigued him so much. "So, what's your favorite?" he asked.

"Don't tell Ali, I really like the deviled crab, but the boiled shrimp are my favorite," Zeke confided. "What your favorite?"

"I love boiled shrimp, too. My dad lives in Louisiana. Every time Mom sent me to live with him, I would beg for him to take me out to a shrimp boil. Most of the time, he'd take me—eventually."

Zeke looked at him with one raised eyebrow, Ace could tell that he was picking up on his screwed-up childhood. He didn't say anything about that, but he asked, "I need to get to know each of you better, and you need to see who I am as well. Do you think it would upset Ali if I took each of you separately for an outing?"

Ace looked at him quietly for a moment as he thought. He searched his face for any inkling of whether he had found one of them lacking in some way. Nothing in his expression gave away any hint of displeasure. Deciding that he might as well ask, Ace said, "Ali and I have been an inseparable team. Have you changed your mind already and only want one of us?"

As if psychic, Ali floated over to join the conversation. She got in on the last of Ace's question. "What's going on? What do you mean, only want one of us?"

"I'd like to get to know each of you individually. I asked Ace if he thought you would be okay with me taking each of you out separately. I'm not talking about dividing you or choosing one of you over the other." Zeke dropped his napkin on the bar and pushed the barely eaten platter away as if he'd lost his appetite. His face was drawn with worry.

Placing her hand over Ace's as he braced himself against the bar, Ali soothed, "I think Ace may have misunderstood. I think it's a superb idea for you to get to know us individually and together." She turned to look at Ace. "I trust you to go out with Zeke by yourself. You won't run away to Tahiti without me, right?"

"I understand that you're a bonded pair. That's exactly who I've been looking for. I would never try to come between the two of you," Zeke said softly, holding Ace's gaze. Without looking, he moved his hand to cover theirs on the bar.

"Honestly?" Ace asked. When Zeke nodded, Ace tried to relax, allowing his shoulders to lower. "I'm sorry. I overreacted."

"Ace has learned not to trust people. Well, other than me. I think he should go first," Ali suggested.

"Deal. You're coming over tomorrow morning to go surfing. If that's still the plan, we'll come up with a time for me to spend with each of you individually." Zeke nodded at Ali as if thanking her.

"Sorry, I think I misunderstood," Ace admitted. Cursing inside, Ace tried to think about how he could make this better. When Ali was called to the other side of the bar, he apologized, "I'm sorry I ruined your lunch." He couldn't quite meet the other man's eyes. He wanted to take back his negative response to what had been a natural question, but something held him back.

"You haven't ruined my lunch. Just gave me time to get a second wind," Zeke said cheerfully. When Ace looked at him in surprise, he continued. "I will work on this shrimp. When you come back, we'll see if I changed my mind about my favorite."

Looking gratefully at Zeke, Ace nodded and moved to check on his other customers. When he had mixed fresh drinks and delivered food to the couple beside Zeke, he returned to talk to the intriguing man who monopolized his attention without even trying. "I'm a jerk sometimes," he confided. Zeke might as well know what he was getting.

"Me, too," Zeke said with a smile. "I bet Ali is, too, at times."

Ace nodded his head vigorously. "Just don't tell her, I told you that."

Zeke laughed and changed the conversation. "I've changed my mind again. These fried oysters rock."

Laughing with relief, Ace agreed, "Maybe those are my favorites, too."

The two bartenders were sad to see Zeke leave. Thankfully, lots of customers distracted them as the evening rush hour began. With their minds occupied with blended drinks and appetizer orders, the two didn't have time to dwell on anything other than taking care of the customers. Before they knew it, they were cleaning up the bar to get ready to leave.

CHAPTER 8

The next morning, Ali and Ace stood at Zeke's front door. It was 7:00 a.m. and time to hit the best waves of the morning. They had discussed time with Zeke before and only realized that maybe it was too early when they arrived. Ali reached out to block Ace's move toward the doorbell.

"What if we're too early?" she hissed.

"He knows what time surfers head out," Ace answered, reaching again for the doorbell.

Smack! This time Ali slapped his arm to make him stop.

"Ouch! Cut it out!"

The sound of the door opening drew both of their attention. "I'm awake. I've been waiting for you. Never wait on the doorstep, no matter what the time is," Zeke corrected them. Wearing only a pair of swim trunks, he grinned at them from the doorway.

"See, Ali!" Ace wrinkled his nose at her.

"I just didn't want to bother you," Ali blurted, ignoring Ace. She let her eyes drift over Zeke's body. Damn, he was in prime shape.

"You could take a picture," Ace teased her. He stepped forward to wrap his arms around Zeke's waist and leaned in to give him a kiss. Turning back to face Ali with his arm casually around Zeke's torso, he added, "I'll be in the picture, too, if you don't think your camera will melt because of the heat."

"Oh, you." Ali ignored him. Ace had focused on getting to Zeke's house as early as possible. She knew he wanted to spend time with the man they hoped was their Daddy. Following his lead, Ali stepped forward to loop her arms around Zeke's neck. Pressing a quick kiss to his lips, she stepped back, but Zeke stopped her.

"That's not a proper good-morning kiss, Little girl," Zeke corrected her. He drew her forward once again with a firm hand cupped around the back of her head. This time, Ali wiggled tightly against him as his mouth explored hers, building heat and desire. When he released her, all Ali could do was hold on and stare at him. All words had vanished from her brain.

"After that, I think we all need to jump into the cold water," Ace commented.

Ali looked down at his pelvis as he adjusted himself in the baggy swim trunks. There is no missing his burgeoning erection. She laughed as the sexual tension shattered. "I'm ready to go when you are."

"I haven't had my coffee yet. I'll rely on the two of you to make sure I don't go to sleep on my board," Zeke teased as he stood back to welcome them inside.

Within minutes, they headed down the stairs with their boards. Laughter and fun rang from their words. Paddling out to the waves, Ace and Ali called greetings to several friends across the water. Almost as if they had agreed on this previously, they didn't invite anyone to join them. Ali wanted Zeke with them. She didn't want to divert his attention to anyone else—not out of the worry, but because she loved spending time with him alone.

The waves began to die out. Ali looked up at the sun and guessed it was around ten o'clock. They'd had a good run. Each had enjoyed at least one spectacular ride. Zeke's skill had surprised her—he must have been outstanding in his late teens and twenties.

"I'm starving," she confessed. "Zeke, do you want to go to the best breakfast place around?"

"Outstanding idea, Ali. I could eat a sand-covered flip-flop," Ace agreed.

"I'd love to treat you both to breakfast. Can we go like this?" Zeke asked, waving a hand to indicate his swim attire.

"We'll all have to put a shirt on. Marie doesn't allow anyone in if they're not covered up," Ace informed him with a laugh. "I've seen some hungry people wearing extraordinary things to eat there."

"You remember that guy that tore a hole in a gigantic map?" Ali asked Ace before turning back to Zeke. "It was one of those that fold up into a rectangle. He just tore a hole in the middle and draped it over his shoulders like a poncho. Marie sat him at the very front table. Everyone still jokes about that guy. Not in a mean way," she clarified. "We'd all have done it, too, if we had been that creative."

"Let's go," Ace urged, heading for the stairs at a brisk trot.

Zeke and Ali followed more sedately. Ali was glad to have a private moment to talk to him. "Daddy? Thanks for understanding when Ace was strange yesterday. You know, about having alone time with us."

"I'm glad you came over to reassure him. I could have done a better job in approaching him with the idea." Zeke rubbed a hand down her spine before linking his fingers with hers.

"He's usually very open to ideas." Ali took several steps in silence before adding, "Our relationship, his and mine, has been the most stable in his life. That's one thing I love about him. I know his commitment to me is strong and deep."

Zeke squeezed her hand. As they reached the stairs, he indicated for her to go first, and he would follow. At the top, Zeke held her back for a moment with a gentle hand around her waist. "Thank you for sharing your insight. I'm looking forward to learning more about you as well."

She knew he understood and accepted Ace the way he was. That was really all you could ask was for someone to care about the real you. Ali hadn't realized that she was holding back a bit of herself. The fear of getting hurt and not having her dreams come true ran deep inside her.

"It will crush me if this doesn't work out," she confessed, meeting his gaze directly.

"Come on, slowpokes! I'm starving here," Ace called from the doorway to Zeke's house.

Acknowledging him with a wave, Zeke quietly suggested to Ali, "Let's make sure it does." He racked his surfboard up in front of Ace's and took care of Ali's. "Okay?"

"Okay," she exhaled.

"Let's go in. I know you need to potty before we go."

"How do you know that?" she asked as they reached the door.

"I'm watching you dance," Zeke shared with a grin.

"I am not!"

"Oh yes, you are!" Ace crowed, standing back to allow her to run through the house to the bathroom.

Good-natured laughter followed her as she darted down the hall. Ali quickly used the toilet, sighing with relief. She wished she could go to the bathroom in the ocean like everybody else did, but it felt wrong. Flushing the toilet, she stopped to wash her hands in the sink.

Ali gasped at the sight of the two sippy cups sitting next to the bathroom faucet. She instantly knew which one was hers. Picking it up, she rotated the cup to look at all the sides. It was decorated with dancing unicorns. Unwilling to put it down, she tucked it under her arm and quickly washed and dried her hands. She tried to open the top, but it was too tight.

"Daddy! Look what I found!" Ali ran to rejoin the men with the sippy cup held over her head. "There's one in there for you, too, Ace!"

Ace immediately headed down the hallway. Ali quickly handed hers to Zeke. "Would you open it for me?" She shifted impatiently as Zeke wrapped his hands around the cup and twisted it open.

"Sorry, Little girl. I should've opened it for you. Would you like some juice?" Zeke asked her with a smile as he laid the two pieces in her eagerly stretched-out hands.

"I love grape juice," she shared distractedly as she rotated the plastic to see the unicorns again.

"Mine has dinosaurs on it," Ace announced as he sped back to join them. He showed Ali his cup with pride. "And it's yellow! That's my favorite color!"

"Better have Daddy help you open it," Ali advised.

"I can do it." Ace dismissed that idea. He tried twisting the top, but it didn't budge. "I think you got a broken one," he reported, handing it to Zeke.

With one easy twist, Zeke opened the top. "Sometimes there are tricks that only Daddies know," he reassured Ace when the young man looked disturbed. "Do you like grape juice as well?" he asked quickly to distract him.

"I love it!"

"Let's go get a couple of juices to go," Zeke suggested. He led the way when both Littles cheered at that suggestion.

When he pulled a bottle of clear juice from the fridge, Ali hesitated before saying, "That's not grape juice, is it?"

"Have you never tried white grape juice?" Zeke asked. When they both shook their heads, he poured a small amount in each and screwed on the top. "Try it, and I'll get you some more if you like it."

"Mmm!" Ali enthusiastically nodded her head. "I love it!"

"Me, too!" Ace chimed in.

Zeke took the cups from them and added more juice to fill them halfway. "That should get you to the restaurant," he suggested. He wrapped an arm around each of their waists and guided them to the door.

Ace was so busy trying to figure out how Zeke opened the lid that he missed a step and stumbled. As he rebalanced, the lid finally popped off, spilling juice over his shirt. Plucking the fabric away from his chest, Ace complained, "Oh, man! I'm all sticky."

"Now you know why I bought clear juice," Zeke laughed. "No problem. Take that shirt off, Ace. I'll run in to grab one of my shirts, and I'll throw it in the washer."

"I'll still be sticky," Ace complained.

Ali knew he needed to get something to eat. Ace was usually even-tempered until he was hungry. Laughing, she ran over to turn on the hose. As Ace handed Zeke his wet shirt, she sprayed him with a blast of cold water. "Now, you're not sticky."

Ace just looked at her in shock as he dripped water onto the sidewalk. Zeke, who had stood back to avoid getting hit by the stream, patted him on the back. "I'll pick up a towel, too, for you to sit on in the car. I'd assume Marie wouldn't like you dripping on her floor either." Both Littles instantly began shaking their heads.

When they finally settled in the car, Zeke looked in the rearview mirror to meet Ace's gaze. "Now you know why I choose clear juice. It's a lot easier on clothing."

Ali turned to look over the passenger seat. She hoped Ace wouldn't be upset with her. To her delight, her best friend was petting the front of the borrowed T-shirt. She understood immediately. Wearing something of their Daddy's was enough fun to wipe away any anger.

Ali glanced at Zeke as she rotated to face the front. She hoped he'd brought plenty of clothes. At this rate they would borrow everything he had—she knew Ace would keep that shirt.

As if reading her mind, Zeke wrapped his fingers around her knee to squeeze slightly. "It's okay. I kind of like having the two of you dressed in my clothes. Now, whoever's riding shotgun has to give Daddy directions," he reminded her.

Pleased to have such an important job, Ali sat up straight in the seat. "Up there at the stoplight, turn left." She took a drink from her unicorn cup before carefully placing it in the holder. There had been enough accidents already.

CHAPTER 9

Ace knocked hesitantly on Zeke's door. He was all alone that morning. When the door opened, he said quickly, "Hi! Ali got tagged to work for a banquet today. I'm afraid you're stuck with me."

Zeke said nothing but stepped out and wrapped his arms around Ace. After hugging him tightly, Zeke took a half step back to press his lips against Ace's. Heat flared instantly between the two men. Ripping his mouth away, Zeke answered, "I'd be stuck with you any day. Come inside," he invited.

They exchanged a second passionate kiss after the door closed. Zeke pushed Ace backward until he was braced against the door. Zeke's body weight pinned him in place as his mouth explored his. Ace wrapped his arms around the older man and held on as Zeke's natural scent filled his senses.

This was so different from kissing Ali. With her, Ace had to be careful to not be too aggressive or too passive. Now, Zeke dominated him. Tethered in place, Ace could respond as he wanted without worry about hurting Zeke. He slid his hands down Zeke's spine to clasp his muscular buttocks and pressed their pelvises together. He could feel Zeke's thick penis growing harder against him. A shiver of desire raced through his body.

When Zeke stepped away, Ace tried to follow but was held at arm's distance. "Turn around," Zeke ordered. The older man's voice was rough.

Instantly, Zeke followed his directions. Pressing his hands against the smooth wooden door, Ace looked over his shoulder. Zeke prowled forward to wrap his arms around Ace's waist. His mouth lowered to the sensitive spot where Ace's shoulder and neck met. There Zeke pressed a fiery kiss against his neck before opening his mouth to bite him.

Freezing in place, Ace felt those white teeth grip his flesh just on the edge of breaking the skin. He groaned at the feel of Zeke's hot tongue sliding over his skin. He rolled his head to the side, silently inviting more. Ace felt like his penis would split open the board shorts he put on that morning. A wordless protest exploded from his lips as Zeke released him.

"Little boy, when this happens, it will be so good. I want you to be ready so you can take me here." Zeke's hand slowly drew a line from between his shoulders down his spine to the divide between his buttocks. Pressing into the material, he pressed his fingers against Ace's body. "Do you want me here?"

"Yes!" Ace arched his back, pushing his ass against Zeke's probing hand. His heart raced, pounding against his chest as he dropped his forehead against the cool wood.

"I want this so bad," he admitted, before whispering, "I'm scared." Ace closed his eyes and wished with all his might that Zeke would be happy with him. That little voice in the back of his head that always warned him of the worst possibility silently screamed, *Please don't let him step away.*

To his relief, Zeke stepped forward to press his erection against that divide. His mouth returned to that sensitive spot, pressing another fervent kiss into Ace's skin like a brand of possession. "Look on the coffee table. Daddy's going to start preparing your bottom."

Turning to look, Ace spotted a metal anal plug next to a tube and a small towel. By reflex, he squeezed his butt. It seemed so thick. *Will it fit?*

Silently, Zeke stepped away from him. Ace watched him walk over to the couch and take a seat. "Come stand in front of me," Zeke calmly directed. Zeke held Ace's gaze until he pushed away from the wall and approached the couch. When Ace got within arm's distance, Zeke placed his hands on each side of his hips and guided Ace to stand between his legs. Hooking his fingers into the top of Ace's bathing suit, Zeke pulled them down to his ankles.

Trapped by the material shackling his legs, Ace teetered, unbalanced. Again Zeke's hands gripped his hips, this time to steady him. "Over my lap, Little boy."

Allowing the powerful hands to guide him, Ace awkwardly leaned over Zeke's thighs. The older man moved him easily into position with his bottom pointing up into the air, and Ace's erection trapped between his spread thighs. Each time he tried to move, his exposed penis brushed against the wiry hair covering Zeke's legs. Ace tried to resist the rough caresses. But his body craved the stimulation. Unable to resist the sensations, Ace flexed his muscles to repeat the movement.

A firm hand pressed on his bottom to stop the slight wiggles. "This is not the time for play, Little boy. Stay very still," Zeke instructed.

The blood rushed to his head. Ace could feel his heart beating quickly. It skipped a beat as Zeke spread his buttocks wide. The sound of lubricant squirting from the tube made him bite his lip. *I don't know if I can do this.*

Ace wanted this so badly. Even if submitting totally to this man was the hardest thing he'd ever done, Ace knew he trusted Zeke. He couldn't imagine allowing anyone else to treat him so intimately. A low groan burst from his lips as Zeke's fingers pressed into his rectum. Spreading the slippery lubricant everywhere, they eventually stilled, implanted deep inside him.

"Good Little boys receive pleasure when they cooperate. Tell me, Ace, do you enjoy the feel of Daddy's fingers inside you?" Zeke's fingers sought that special place inside his rectum and stroked over his prostate.

Thrusting his hips forward, Ace could only focus on the rough sound of Zeke's voice and the feel of those fingers stretching and invading him. Again, one of his Daddy's hands stabilized him, stopping his motion. Zeke's next words made him beg.

"Daddy will be here soon. Hot and deep inside you. It's going to make you feel so good. That is if you're a good Little boy," he promised.

"I can be good! I promise. Daddy, please!"

"You'll wear the plug first. Daddy will decide when it's time." His fingers slid from Ace's body.

When Ace tried to press his bottom backward, he learned that it was important to be careful in this position. *Smack! Smack! Smack!* Zeke's hand landed sharply on his tender skin. Ace froze in place and bit his lip to keep from crying out.

Almost immediately, he felt the cold metal tip of the anal plug press against his puckered opening. That coldness invaded his tight passage, making him shiver and tighten his muscles in reaction. "Daddy! Daddy! Daddy!" Ace chanted as the burn of his stretching channel pushed his limits.

"Just a little more. You can take it for Daddy, can't you?" Zeke encouraged him. With one more push, the widest section of the plug entered, and that tight ring of muscles clenched around the smaller neck as the thick base settled into place.

Panting in reaction to the invasion, Ace tightened his muscles around the plug. He could feel it inside. The cold metal chilling his warm passage, it pressed against something that felt so good. He closed his eyes as his mind tried to imagine it was Zeke's thick erection inside him.

When the older man's hand wrapped around Ace's shaft, a low aroused moan fell from his lips. As the delicious sensations whirled around him, Ace moved automatically as Zeke's hands helped him shift to sit on his Daddy's lap. Cradled against one shoulder, Ace watched in fascination as Zeke pulled firmly against his erection.

Held against Zeke's warm body, his weight settled on that thick plug. Each stroke jarred his position, making the invader move inside him. Ace could only stare at the muscular hand moving on his cock. More aroused than he'd ever been in his life, Ace's body exploded into the small towel that Zeke held.

"Daddy!" burst from Ace's lips as he clung to Zeke's strength. His breath came fast and hard. Ace could feel his heart racing inside his chest.

Zeke began rocking Ace gently on his lap as his arms gathered his Little close. That inserted anal plug moved inside Ace to extend his pleasure. Zeke held him as if there was no limit on time. His Daddy was here for him. "What a very good Little boy," Zeke praised him softly.

As Ace's heart slowed, Zeke pressed a kiss against his temple. "Daddy will be right back," he whispered. As Ace processed his words, Zeke half lifted, half scooted his bottom onto the couch. Ace watched him stand. Immediately, he missed the warm embrace.

Ace wrapped his arms around himself as he watched Zeke enter the kitchen. The sound of the refrigerator opening and closing, followed by the buzz of the microwave, pissed him off. Clenching his fists, Ace sat up. The couch creaked underneath him, drawing Zeke's attention.

"Stay where you are, Little boy. I can tell from your red face that you're angry." The ding of the microwave interrupted him. Zeke disappeared from view again to retrieve whatever was heating in the microwave.

Ace could hear a sloshing of liquid. *What is he doing?* His eyes fixed on the entrance to the kitchen. Quickly, Zeke appeared carrying a bottle that he was shaking gently. The breath caught in Ace's chest. Zeke had listened and had gotten supplies to fulfill his fantasies.

Taking a seat, Zeke regathered him into his arms. He cradled him at a slight incline. "Here, Little boy. Let Daddy take care of you." Zeke brushed the large nipple against Ace's lips. When he hesitated, afraid of looking silly, Zeke reassured him, "There's only Daddy and his Little boy here. Try your Daddy's special formula. I'm eager to know if you like it."

He opened his mouth to allow Zeke to slide the tip inside. A droplet of sweet liquid landed on his tongue. Instinctively, he sucked. "Mmm!" The nipple felt weird in his mouth, but the formula was so delicious that he continued to drink. Ace quickly adjusted to the strange feel. He looked up at Zeke to make sure he was doing the right thing.

"Daddy's glad you like the formula. It's good for Little boys and girls. I think my Little boy will need special attention from Daddy often. I want you to be strong and happy."

Ace nodded, eager to imagine having an intimate time with Zeke. He was glad this first time it was just him and his Daddy. He loved having Ali around, but having all of Zeke's attention was amazing. Ace closed his eyes as Zeke began brushing one hand through his blond hair. The stroke on his scalp both comforted and made him feel cherished. He exhaled, relaxing fully.

D*amn, I love him. How did this happen so fast?* Zeke stared down at the sleeping Little in his arms. He'd had to travel a distance to find the proper supply of products to care for his Littles. It was all worthwhile now.

What am I going to do if they decide that I'm not the right Daddy for them? Or, if they're not willing to leave all that is familiar, to start a new life with me in SANCTUM? Zeke forced his doubts from his head. He knew that they were right for him. He needed to ensure that they had all the reassurance and special attention to help them make the right decision. It had to be Ali and Ace's choice.

Holding his precious armful, Zeke formulated a plan. His Little boy and girl would need a series of steps before moving permanently. The builders assured him that in two weeks they would finish his house. He'd make a call to Gordon's, the most renowned supplier of everything Little.

Perhaps Benton Gordon's Little girl, Charlotte, would lend her talents to decorating his home. Benton was intrigued by the community and had mentioned that perhaps a vacation home would be good for his Little and himself. This would be an excellent excuse for them to visit.

Smiling at the sleeping Little cradled in his arms, Zeke allowed himself to enjoy this quiet time. The future was full of promise. He'd make sure that both Ace and Ali felt comfortable in making this life-changing decision. That's what a Daddy's for, isn't it?

CHAPTER 10

Dragging herself out of the employee entrance, Ali took a breath of the fresh air. She'd been trapped in the banquet room for hours. It had been a fascinating day, for sure. The attendees of the Wedded Bliss marriage workshop had kept her hopping all day long. Ali had understood why they needed an extra glass of wine or scotch to make it through the frank conversations.

She'd learned a lot in the short segments she'd been able to pay attention to. Ali understood why the manager had chosen her to serve. She accepted and appreciated everyone. At first, the attendees had glanced back at her frequently to judge her reaction to the activities and confessions. However, soon, she blended into the environment and only gained their attention when she could provide a fresh beverage. They'd appreciated this—her tip jar overflowed.

Now, all she wanted to do was sit on her Daddy's lap. She heard lots of problems and watched couples reconnect with each other. Ali swore she'd never lose that precious connection with those she loved. Now, she needed the reassurance that Ace and Zeke felt the same way.

Beep! Beep! Ali spun to see Zeke's car waiting for her a short distance away. The two men inside waved enthusiastically. She hurried to join them. As she got close, Ace jumped out of the passenger seat and invited her to sit in the middle on the bench seat.

Feeling her heavy thoughts float away, she slid in. Before she could say hi, Zeke pulled her close to press an ardent kiss to her lips. Ali felt Ace slide in beside her. When Zeke leaned back, Ace wrapped a hand around her thigh to draw her attention. Turning to him, Ali lifted her lips to accept his kiss.

"Wow! What a welcome!" Ali enthused. She studied Ace's face to see how the alone time had gone with Zeke. Her longtime friend looked more relaxed than he had in a long time. "So, what have you all been up to?" she asked curiously.

Putting the car in drive, Zeke drove out of the crowded parking lot. "We've been preparing Ace's bottom for our lovemaking," he announced.

"Daddy!" Ace protested in embarrassment.

Ali turned to stare at Ace. To her amusement, his face turned bright pink. She'd never seen him so flustered. Stifling a laugh that threatened to burst from her, Ali linked her fingers with his and squeezed. Ace shifted slightly, and she saw a flash of discomfort.

"Do you have something in your bottom?" she blurted before clapping one hand over her mouth. Ace's face turned a darker red, and he nodded.

"I'll start training your bottom as well." Zeke shared this as if it was a normal everyday conversation while driving down the road. "It's important for Littles to be well prepared."

A wave of heat seared through Ali's body. She gripped Ace's hand tighter as a scene developed in her imagination. Many times she'd dreamed of their sexual relationship with their Daddy. Now with the face to fill in for the Daddy, who had previously been in shadows, everything became real. She felt herself becoming wet and squeezed her thighs together.

Ignoring the conversation that floated over her between Zeke and Ace, Ali concentrated on the mental images. When they pulled up outside their small apartment, Ali forced herself to focus on the present. "So? What are we doing?"

"Ace suggested that you would like to take a shower after your shift. Then before you put on your clothing to have dinner, I'll place an anal plug in your bottom as well," Zeke shared.

"In my bottom?" she repeated, mind boggled. Ali responded mechanically as the men opened their doors. She put her hand in Ace's when he offered it and allowed him to help her glide to the edge of the seat.

As they walked to the apartment building door, Zeke wrapped his arm around her waist as Ace held her hand. The area was quiet. Too early for most people to be home. The trio didn't pass anyone before reaching their door. Once inside, Ali asked quickly, "Will it hurt?"

Zeke pulled her tight against his chest for a quick hug before picking her up in his arms. Carrying her to the battered sofa, Zeke took a seat with Ali held in his arms. "I will never hurt you, Little girl. That's the entire purpose of the plug. It will stretch your body to accept Ace's or my penis. Have you ever had anal sex?"

"No," Ali answered with a wavering voice. "We tried once, but it was too painful," she admitted.

"I'm sorry," Zeke said, hugging her close. "Sex should be about pleasure, not about pain. Let's get you ready to enjoy everything," he suggested.

Ali looked uncertainly at Ace, who hovered next to them. He immediately reassured her, "It's not that bad. Daddy knows how to make everything feel good."

"Okay," she said in a trembling voice.

"That's my brave girl. Go take a shower. No playing without us," Zeke instructed as he lifted her up to stand.

"No playing?" she repeated in confusion, then felt her face heat. He was referring to masturbation.

"There are no secrets between a Little and her Daddy," Zeke reminded her.

Nodding, Ali fled into the bathroom. She closed the door behind her and leaned against the cool wood. *How does he know everything?*

Stripping off her clothing, Ali turned on the water and stepped immediately into the cold spray. It wiped all the thoughts from her mind as she shivered. Ali rubbed the bar of soap briskly over her skin and rotated to rinse herself clean. By the time she cleaned her face, the water had warmed. Finally, she rubbed the slippery cleanser between her legs and buttocks. Rinsing away the signs of her desire,

Ali quickly finished, steadfastly following the directions that Zeke had given her.

She stepped out of the shower stall to find Zeke holding the towel open for her. Surprised, she bolted forward to cover her nudity. He'd seen her naked, but only when the three of them had been together in the shower. Now having him dressed, she felt more vulnerable.

Zeke wrapped a towel around her and pulled her in to lean against his body. He held her in place as she regained her composure. "I'm sorry to startle you, Little girl. I'll make sure you hear me in the future. Will you allow me to take care of you?" he asked softly.

Lifting the corner of the towel to dry her face, Ali whispered, "Yes."

"Thank you," he said as he began to brush the towel gently over her wet skin. When he squatted down to dry her legs, Zeke leaned forward to press his lips tenderly against her mound, sending a wave of desire through her body.

Automatically, she widened her legs, inviting his touch. When Zeke just chuckled and continued his task, Ali sighed in regret. That small sound also pleased Zeke. As he stood, he pulled her close to his body and kissed her sweetly.

Lifting his lips, he instructed, "Go put your hands on the vanity and lean over." When she didn't move quickly but looked at him in surprise, Zeke urged her on with a sharp swat on her bottom.

As Ali walked toward the mirror, she noted the jar of lubricant and silver anal plug waiting. Shooting a glance over her shoulder, Ali hesitated. When she saw the stern look on his face, she scurried forward and assumed the position that he had requested.

"Widen your legs, sweetheart."

Quickly she followed his directions. As she watched in the mirror, Ali saw him open the lubricant and scoop a finger full of the thick mixture. Zeke turned to her and ran a hand down her spine to her buttocks. Holding her gaze in the mirror, he parted her cheeks, dabbed the cold mixture onto her small, tight opening. She raised up onto her toes as his finger immediately began pushing through that clenched ring of muscle to glide in deep.

"Relax, Ali. Daddy will make sure you're ready to take him or Ace here. Does it turn you on to think of having both of us inside you at the same time?"

"Yes," she moaned, unable to tear her gaze from his. The reflection in the mirror made things more real. Appealing to her need for submission, Ali felt Little. She couldn't argue with the fact that her Daddy was in charge. He held his finger deeply implanted inside her until she followed his instructions and forced herself to relax her muscles.

"Good girl," he praised.

A thrill went through her. She wanted Zeke to be pleased with her. The finger inside her moved. Ali closed her eyes as the sensations overwhelmed her. After several strokes, the finger withdrew. Her eyes flashed open to watch him pick up the silver plug and dip it into the thick mixture.

That caressing hand once again stroked down her back. This time, he held her buttocks spread wide as he touched the cold metal to her opening. Without giving her time to adjust, Zeke pushed the plug inside. Slowly but surely, it breeched the tight opening. Ali rose to her toes once again as the thickest part entered her body. Zeke did not pause but continued to press it deeper inside.

Her heels dropped to the floor as the plug settled into place, the immense pressure disappearing at the entrance. Within seconds, the plug moved once again. This time, it slid outward. Once again, her eyes met his in the mirror. She watched him smile and knew his treatment had just begun.

Zeke reached a hand around her body to trace her labia down into the wetness gathering between her legs. His fingers explored her delicate, pink folds as he pushed the anal plug back into place. "Can you come for Daddy?" he suggested.

"Daddy?" she asked, before confessing, "This should not feel this good."

"All that gives pleasure is good," he reassured her as he tapped lightly on her clitoris. It did not take much.

That last bit of stimulation pushed Ali over the brink into a massive climax. She fell forward to drop her head onto her hands, pushing her bottom toward him. The plug continued to glide slowly in and out to prolong her pleasure. Finally, he allowed it to rest inside her.

Ali released a shuddering sigh as he lifted her from the vanity and rotated her to hold Ali in his arms. She clung to him for stability as she navigated the last of the waves of pleasure. When her body finally calmed, she raised her head from his shoulders, "I didn't know it could be like that."

"Together, we will explore what everyone enjoys. Promise me you will always tell me the truth. I can't make things better if you don't talk to me. That doesn't mean that I won't push you, because I will," he warned with a serious look.

"Yes, Daddy. I promise."

A tentative knock on the door made them both turn. Zeke knew that Ace wanted to join them but didn't want to interrupt Ali's private time with him. "Come in, Ace," Zeke welcomed him. When the Little boy entered, Ali flew into his arms. Zeke followed to wrap them both in his embrace.

"So good," Ali whispered.

"I know," Ace agreed, then kissed her tenderly before offering his lips to Zeke.

CHAPTER 11

That evening, Ali and Ace packed a bag and left their small apartment to move in with Zeke. Neither knew how long they could spend with this amazing man, but they were determined to be with him as much as possible. Thankfully, he felt exactly the same way.

"Let's watch a movie tonight," Zeke suggested. "I'd love to spend the evening here alone with the two of you. But first, it's time for dinner." He shepherded them into the kitchen and guided each Little to a seat. In front of Ali and Ace sat a colorful gift bag with a plume of tissue paper.

Ace immediately ripped the filler out of the opening of the sack to look inside. With a cry, he pulled out a large bib with a surfing bear on the front with a matching, colorful sippy cup. "This is so neat!"

Turning the sack to look at each side, Ali appreciated the outside wrapping before slowly unveiling the gifts inside. Peeking in the top, she withdrew a pink bib with an animated unicorn and a matching cup with dollies and unicorns. She hugged both to her heart as she thanked Zeke. "I love them!"

Zeke dropped a kiss on both of their heads as he fastened the bib around each Little's neck. Filling the sippy cups with ice-cold milk, he set them in front of them. "Let Daddy get dinner on the table."

Zeke bustled off and worked in the kitchen. He had placed several dishes in the oven to heat. Ace inhaled appreciatively and rubbed his tummy, a quiet signal to Ali that he was hungry. She nodded immediately. Even that slight movement reminded her of the device inside her.

As she shifted uncomfortably on the inserted plug, Ace whispered, "It gets better."

"Really? Can't you feel it?"

"Of course, silly." Ace made a funny face at her, which caused both Littles to giggle.

Zeke carried a casserole dish full of macaroni and cheese over to the table. He smiled at the sound of their laughter, saying, "That's the sound I want to hear for the rest of my life."

"Really?" Ali repeated herself. "Don't you think you'd get tired of us?" she probed, holding her breath in anticipation of his answer. She wanted to hear it, but she was afraid. What if he didn't mean that? People made statements like that all the time and didn't really want them to happen.

Immediately, Zeke walked to the back of her chair to wrap his arms around her. "I never say anything that I don't mean. I hope to convince the two of you to come with me to SANCTUM. Perhaps we can talk about that over dinner?"

"I'd like that," she answered, surprising even herself. Ali didn't have anything to keep her in this town. She'd stayed because Ace was there, and she had a job. All this time, Ali felt as if she was only existing. Perhaps she would thrive somewhere else. As he turned away to bring things to the table, she looked at Ace, trying to read his expression.

"Would you mind moving away?" he whispered.

"No," she answered honestly. "What about you?"

"I seesawed back and forth between Mom and Dad's so much growing up. I don't really think this is where I'm supposed to be. I called it home because you're here," he admitted.

They both looked at each other in the sudden realization that there was really nothing holding them back. Their paltry amount of possessions and clothing in their furnished apartment would all fit in the back of Zeke's SUV. Ali felt her lips spread in a wide smile and saw the expression mirrored on Ace's face. That feeling of freedom to do whatever they chose to do was intoxicating. She returned his nod. They both agreed.

After adding a generous scoop of macaroni and cheese, grilled chicken cut into small pieces, and asparagus spears to each Little's plate, Zeke filled his own. The Littles were not allowed to pass the dishes. They were too hot and too heavy for them to handle.

Picking up a green stalk, Ali bit the tip off and hummed in appreciation. The lemon pepper seasoning made it taste fantastic. "Ace, try this. It's the best asparagus I've ever eaten!"

He looked very skeptically at the vegetable. "I don't think I like asparagus."

"You don't like that stuff in the cans. It's mushy and awful. I'm not joking. It's safe." Ali took another big bite to prove to him she really liked it.

Cautiously, Ace picked one up and tried a tiny sample. Immediately his eyebrows lifted comically, and Ali laughed. Taking a bigger bite, Ace spoke with his mouth open. "This is yummy!"

"Don't talk with your mouth full, Little boy," Zeke reprimanded nicely. "I'll take that as a super compliment. I'm glad you like your Daddy's cooking."

A hush descending over the table as everyone enjoyed the delicious food. As Zeke ladled a second helping of macaroni onto Ace's plate, he asked, "Would you all be interested in hearing about SANCTUM?"

"Is it like a town?" Ace asked.

"SANCTUM began with a group of men who all wished for a place where their Littles could be themselves, so it's like a private, invitation-only town. Pooling our money, we invested in a large plot of land and enclosed it in a protective fence to keep everyone inside secure."

The Littles looked at each other. Ali knew Ace's thoughts mirrored hers. There, they could be Little all the time without worrying about others judging them. Leaning forward, she asked, "Do a lot of people live there?"

"One by one, the men are building their homes and settling on the land. Shelby was the first to move in with her Daddies. Now, Lindy, Priscilla, Poppy, Rita, and Nicky have all settled there too with their Daddies. Hunter and Samantha come to visit often, but they do not live there full-time," Zeke explained.

"That's a lot of Littles! I'm glad there's a couple of guys." Ace looked relieved.

"I have a feeling there'll be more little boys coming to live in SANCTUM soon. You'll like Nicky. He's a rodeo rider. And Hunter's amazing! He's a tattoo artist and very talented," Zeke shared.

A look of concern floated across Ace's face. "I'm not really good at anything," he admitted.

Ali opened her mouth to argue but fell quiet when Zeke reached across to cover Ace's hand, fidgeting on the table. "Little boy, you are good at a million things. You make both me and Ali happy and entertained. I've seen your sand creations. The people that sit at your end of the bar love you and come back time and time again. You are one of those souls that attract others. I treasure you in my life and am so glad I found you."

"You're not just trying to make me feel better, are you?" Ace asked, apprehension showing on his face.

When Zeke shook his head, Ali added, "Can I just say, ditto? Because that's exactly how I feel, too." That caused both men to laugh, breaking the tension.

"Shelby has two Daddies? That means nobody will think we're weird to have two Littles with one Daddy?" Ali figured she might as well ask. She'd always hated being the one kid in school who didn't have a mom and dad to come to programs and open house. She'd always been good, so her teachers would never call home and discover that her parents hadn't liked her enough to stick around.

"I don't think anyone would think anything is weird at SANCTUM. The Littles, of course, are glad to have new playmates," Zeke reassured her.

"Would it be possible for us to go for a visit?" Ali suggested, observing Zeke's face to judge his reaction.

"We can go for a visit anytime you like," Zeke agreed. "I'm

supposed to be here for two weeks. Let's spend that time together and see how you feel. I don't need any reassurance that you're my Littles, but I want you to be sure I'm the right Daddy. This is a big decision."

Ali looked at Ace, and when he nodded, she spoke for them. "We'd like that."

The talk ceased for a few seconds as everyone mentally reviewed the conversation. Laughter replaced that silence when Ace held out his plate one more time. "Could I have more mac and cheese?" Zeke happily filled his plate with several more spoonfuls.

When bedtime rolled around, Zeke helped his Littles prepare for bed. With clean teeth and faces, Ali and Ace took turns leaning over the bed to present their bottoms. Zeke slowly removed the anal plug, making sure that they felt every fraction of an inch as it slid from their bodies. He made sure to wash them and set them on the vanity next to the jar of lubricant. His actions demonstrated to Ali and Ace that they would wear the devices again—and soon.

"Ali, please sit on the bed to wait for just a moment," Zeke instructed. He waited until she was in place before he began undressing Ace. Brushing his hands away as the Little attempted to help, Zeke lifted the T-shirt over his head and pushed his shorts over Ace's hips.

Lifting the corner of the covers, he told Ace, "You get the middle today. Tomorrow you get the right side, and Ali gets the center spot." Without any questions, Ace got into bed and into position. Repeating the pattern with Ali, he removed her clothing and tucked her tenderly in bed.

"Daddy has a few things to do. Then, a bit later, I will come in to sleep with you. Remember, keep your hands to yourself. Your pleasure belongs to me." When they both nodded their agreement, he turned off the lights and closed the door.

"I'll never be able to go to sleep this early," Ace complained.

"Be good. Daddy might decide that he doesn't want us," Ali hissed.

"I won't ever decide that," Zeke called through the door. He listened in delight at the frantic shhhs that followed his words. He had to steel himself from joining the adorable Littles.

A Daddy knew that rules like a steady bedtime and brushing one's teeth gave a Little boy and girl the stability they needed to relax into a lifestyle. For him, he just needed them. His life definitely would not be the same. It would be so much more.

CHAPTER 12

The next morning, Zeke woke up in the middle of the bed. Ali was draped over the left side of his body with her head on his chest. Meanwhile, he was bracketed on the other side by Ace, who had pinned him in place with a possessive leg thrown over his. Zeke's first thought was that he wanted this every morning. He raised his arm draped around Ali's shoulders and brushed the hair away from her face.

"Daddy? Is it time to wake up?"

"It's very early, Little girl. How did you get over here?" Zeke asked, leaning down to kiss her warmly. His heart beat just a bit faster when he lifted his lips from hers.

"Am I in trouble? I was too far away from you. Ace wouldn't move over and let me take his spot, so I just went around the bed and climbed in next to you. Can't you be in the middle?" she asked, lifting herself up onto one elbow.

"I vote we all move around. I want to sleep next to both of you, and I can only do that if I'm in the middle," Ace mumbled. His words were heavy as he fought off his sleepiness.

"He's not a morning person, Daddy," Ali confided. Ace didn't argue. He just nodded his head in agreement.

Enchanted by his sleepy Little, Zeke leaned over to capture his lips. Still halfway in slumbers, Ace's eager response to his kiss delighted Zeke. The Little boy rolled over to look at Ali. Without a single word, the two began to kiss and caress their Daddy's body. Captivated by their desire to please him, Zeke responded eagerly to their touch.

When Ali's fingers slowly traced a path down the center of his torso, Zeke inhaled deeply, urging her on. "Please, Little girl. I need your touch." As she scooted lower in the bed to wrap her hand around his rigid erection, Zeke pulled Ace close to capture his lips in aggressive kisses.

Feeling his Little girl shift in bed, Zeke guessed that Ali had sat up to watch. Zeke knew immediately when Ali's fingers wrapped around Ace's shaft. The young man moaned deeply into his mouth before ripping his lips from Zeke's to look down their bodies.

"Holy crap! That's so hot." Ace expressed precisely what they all were thinking at the sight of her caressing two thick erections.

Ali winked at them before scrambling to kneel between them. Leaning over, she tasted Ace's penis before turning to Zeke's and brushing her tongue across that broad head. Both men groaned in unison. Their hands reached out to caress her shoulders and any other part of her body that they could reach, trying to return the pleasure. They also couldn't resist touching each other.

Within minutes, Zeke sat up fully to pull Ali away from her kissing and nibbling. "No more, Little girl. I need you up here, where I can touch you completely." With Ali in the middle, the men leaned over to kiss a trail to her small breasts. Their fingers tweaked and rolled her nipples while their mouths explored the sensitive underside of her breasts.

When Ali squirmed in between them, Zeke rolled to the nightstand and removed two packets and a small bottle of lubricant from the drawer. "Daddy can only enter one of you. Do you want to decide?" Ace and Ali shook their heads. They wouldn't make that choice. "How many miles is it from here to SANCTUM?" Zeke asked.

They looked at him blankly. Zeke could tell they weren't prepared for a quiz in the middle of sex. After several seconds, Ace blurted, "We don't know. You've never told us."

"Exactly. Guess."

"Three hundred," Ali guessed.

"One thousand," Ace countered.

"It's about eleven hundred miles from here. Ace wins—he's in the middle." Zeke laughed as the Little boy cheered before his face showed lust and nervousness. It appeared he'd just figured out that meant his Daddy would be taking his bottom.

To distract Ace, Zeke leaned forward to kiss him hard to help the passion overrule his jitters. Zeke tore open one condom packet. "First, condoms to protect each other. I bet a Little girl would help us." With a quick nod, Ali's nimble fingers jumped back and forth between erections to help. Both men kissed her deeply to thank her. She glowed under their praise.

"Little boy slide your penis into Ali and then freeze," Zeke directed, smoothing his hands over their bodies as he helped Ace move to cage Ali underneath his body. Her hands smoothed over his chest with the ease of someone who has loved her partner well. Ace's mouth took hers in a passionate kiss.

Zeke didn't think he could get any harder, but his body proved him wrong. He watched his two Littles enjoy each other's body with heartfelt approval. How did he get so lucky to find these two? Sitting back slightly, his mind attempted to capture the images of that moment. *I don't want to forget this—ever!*

When Ace slowly entered Ali, Zeke could tell by their faces how much control it took not to move. Quickly, he moved into position behind Ace. With one hand, he prepared Ace to accept him. Applying lubricant generously to that tight ring of muscles that clenched and relaxed before him, Zeke squirted additional fluid into his tight channel. This first time was essential to ensure his Little boy's pleasure.

He pressed his erection into the groove of Ace's buttocks. Sliding back and forth past that small opening, Zeke drew out the anticipation as he moved his other hand to caress between her thighs, tracing their connection. Instantly, his Littles moaned in reaction to the intimate touch. Leaning over Ace, he growled, "Together!"

Zeke fit himself against Ace's entrance. Slowly, he pressed into his heat. Ace's head reared back in reaction to his invasion. He paused to make sure that his Little felt only pleasure.

"No, don't stop. Please, don't stop!" his Little begged.

Relieved, Zeke continued to ease his shaft inside. His movement pressed Ace deeper inside Ali's channel. He felt his Little boy shake in reaction to the overwhelming sensations flooding his body. Wrapping one arm around Ace's muscular abdomen, Zeke stabilized his position by providing support before he glided out.

Quickly, the trio fell into an enticing pattern. Zeke's thrusts drove Ace into Ali, and his withdrawals drew his Little boy's body backward. Zeke experimented with speeds and movements, carefully observing Ali's facial expressions and Ace's reactions. Their bodies were quickly coated with sweat as the heat built between and around them.

Sliding against each other, the three sought to lavish each other with pleasure. Ali's hands caressed both male bodies above her, touching Zeke and Ace wherever she could. Zeke ran his free hand over the muscular expanse of Ace's back and fondled Ali's body to tantalize her. Zeke pushed the pressure of making this first time memorable out of his mind. Their bonding would occur only if all concentrated on this—the feel of the three of them together.

Ace's movements quickened. Zeke could feel his Little boy's rectum tightening around his shaft and knew that Ace was struggling to postpone his climax. Increasing the speed of his strokes, Zeke drove powerfully into him. With a cry, Ace pumped desperately into Ali's body. Almost simultaneously, her voice blended with his to announce their pleasure. Zeke surrendered to the ironclad grip around his penis and shouted into the room.

When the sensations calmed, Zeke eased Ace to the side. Pulling Ali into sandwich the Little boy between them, Zeke smoothed his hands over their bodies. He leaned over each to kiss them tenderly. "My Littles, I treasure you."

"Did I do okay?" Ace asked, rotating his head to look at each of them.

"Did you feel my orgasm?" Ali whispered. "How did you support yourself above me? I would have collapsed in a few minutes."

"Daddy helped hold me up. I didn't want to hurt you," Ace rushed to say. He peeked back at Zeke with an uncertain expression.

Zeke simply cupped his jaw and drew him forward to press a soft kiss to his lips. "I knew finding my Littles would be amazing. I was not expecting to feel all of this. Joining my body to yours, and through you to Ali, exceeded all my dreams and fantasies. Thank you," he reassured Ace before leaning over his body to exchange a gentle kiss with Ali.

When Ace's stomach growled ferociously in a few minutes, Ali and Zeke laughed, breaking the cocoon of satisfaction that had enwrapped their bodies and minds. "Sounds like I need to feed my Littles."

"We can help!" Ali enthused.

Rolling out of bed, Zeke reached a hand to assist Ali out of bed. "What would you like to eat? Scrambled eggs or pancakes?"

"Pancakes!" the Littles answered in unison.

CHAPTER 13

Days of happiness together followed. Ali and Ace continued to work at the bar while spending as much time as possible with their Daddy. When the bar cleared and they prepped their stations for the next wave of thirsty customers, the two Littles enjoyed talking together to make plans.

"Ali, have you looked at the calendar? We've already spent a week with Zeke. That means we only have seven more days before he leaves." Ace freaked out a bit as he sliced lemons for the evening's garnishes.

"I know. I've been keeping track of the days, too. He didn't say anything about taking us with him for the last couple of days. Do you think he's changed his mind?" Ali suggested with tears in her eyes. They'd given her the task of slicing onions for the house salads. If she was honest, she had to admit there was more than the root vegetable's scent that was making her cry.

"I don't think so. Zeke's always been very definite that we are his Littles," Ace tried to reassure her.

"Is it okay if I ask?" she double-checked with Ace. "I don't want to come off as needy or clingy."

"You're a Little. You're supposed to want to cling to your Daddy. I totally think you should talk to him. I'm supposed to get off an hour earlier than you are tonight. Let's ask the manager on duty tonight if I can stay for you, and you could leave first. Then you could go talk to Daddy alone."

"Are you sure you don't mind?"

"Not at all. You can ask to reassure me, too." Ace grinned at her. "I win either way."

P arking their battered car in the driveway, Ali noticed the pizza delivery vehicle pulled to the curb out front. It was empty. Ali hurried to the front door and let herself in quietly. The smell of hot pizza filled the air, and she noticed two cardboard boxes sitting on the coffee table in the living room. A murmur of voices came from the kitchen.

Something inside her kept Ali from calling out. She walked to the doorway and found Zeke kneeling down in front of Jamie. Instantly, she was jealous. As she watched, Zeke peeled the backing off an adhesive bandage and applied it to an oozing scrape on Jamie's knee.

She opened her mouth to call a greeting, but the words froze in her throat as Jamie leaned forward to wrap her arms around the back of Zeke's neck. Pulling him forward, she pressed a kiss against his lips. A small sound of protest slipped from Ali's lips, drawing Zeke's attention.

His eyes warmed to see her before showing concern as he pushed the young woman away. When Ali whirled and fled back to the front door, she could hear Zeke calling her name. Ignoring his pleas for her to stop, she jumped into her car and turned the ignition key with desperate speed. Racing out of the parking spot, Ali threw it into drive as Zeke emerged from the house.

Her last vision was of Jamie wrapping her hands around his shoulders to slow him down. Her touch appeared sure and practiced. *How long has this been going on?* Ali hit the top of the steering wheel and cursed aloud. She'd hated Jamie throughout high school. The aggressive teenager had pursued Ace at every turn. Now, she had captured Zeke's heart.

Fat tears cascaded down her cheeks. Blinking furiously to maintain her focus on the road, Ali drove to a remote spot just outside of town. She and Ace had discovered the hidden location years ago. She didn't know if Zeke or Jamie would follow her. She needed time alone to think.

Hiding out until Ace could leave, Ali had almost gotten to the restaurant when she glimpsed Zeke's car turning into the parking lot several vehicles ahead of her. She texted Ace to go through the side door rather than through the back with the other employees.

Automatically following her directions, he ran through the adjacent parking lot to meet her. As he jumped into the car, Ali took off and retraced her path. Knowing that she would begin crying as soon as she recounted what had happened, Ali tried to hide her feelings from the man who knew her best.

After one look at her face, Ace demanded, "What's wrong? Why are we using our emergency plan?"

"I'm going to our spot. I'll explain there." Continuing to drive, Ali watched the road intently to avoid meeting Ace's gaze and to make sure she didn't run off the asphalt. Finally, she parked the car under the sheltering trees. Throwing herself into Ace's arms, she allowed the tears to fall once again.

"Ali, sweetheart? What happened? Why are we hiding from Daddy?" he demanded. His hands wrapped around her body to pull her from behind the wheel into his arms.

"I caught him!" Ali sobbed. "He was taking care of Jamie. I can't believe he's trying out other Littles. Do you think he wants to replace me with her?"

"No way, Ali. You misunderstood. What happened?"

Ali recounted how she'd walked in on Zeke as he tended Jamie's knee and the young woman's kiss. "She always tries to ruin everything. You already knew what a conniver she was. You didn't fall for her lies. But Daddy doesn't know how bad she really is!"

"Daddy isn't going to be deceived either, Ali. He's too smart—and he's been searching for a Little boy and girl. That's us!"

"Or you and Jamie," Ali choked out between sobs.

"One, I'm not interested in Jamie. Two, Daddy's not interested in Jamie."

"He could have just handed her the bandage. Why did he have to invite her in and put it on for her?"

"I'm calling Daddy," Ace announced, pulling his phone from his back pocket. Evading Ali's attempts to grab the phone and ignoring her pleas for him to stop, Ace touched the screen to connect with his Daddy.

"Ace! Thank goodness you called. I've been looking for Ali all night. Do you know where she is? I just called the hospital to double-check that she wasn't in an accident," Zeke recounted in a rush of frantic words. He dropped the pink plastic sword he'd been clutching on the coffee table.

"She's here with me, and she's uninjured. I think you two need to talk," Ace shared with his gaze locked with Ali's as she shook her head to refuse.

"Please. I want to talk to both of you," Zeke readily agreed. "Can you get her here?"

"Yes, I'll get her there. Then, it's up to you to figure out how to solve this, Daddy. She's not listening to me," Ace confided.

"You get her here. I'll take it from there."

With that, Ace disconnected to tell Ali, "This is all just a big miscommunication. We're going to Daddy's to talk."

"I don't want to talk to him. Just drop me off at the apartment," she demanded.

"You're going to meet with Daddy for me. This is our chance to have a Daddy together. You owe me that much. If you run away, you take away my Daddy, too. If he was messing with Jamie, I need to know that he's not my Daddy either." Ace twisted the events that Ali had recounted to him to show the impact on him—not in a selfish way. He knew that Ali wouldn't want him to be unhappy either.

She stared at him. Ace could see the wheels inside of her head moving as she digested his request. Finally, she whispered, "I don't want to be hurt, Ace. I want him to be our Daddy so much. What if he doesn't want me?"

"You have to talk to him."

"I know." Ali threw herself against Ace's body and burst into tears on his shoulder. "I'm so scared!"

"Don't forget—Daddy needs you, too." He was pleased to see a glimmer of hope in Ali's eyes. "Scoot over and let me drive. You're too upset." With practiced ease, the two switched places inside the car and Ace drove back to the rental house where they had been so happy. "Please let it all be okay," he chanted inside.

When Ace turned the last corner, their searching eyes noted the delivery car had disappeared. Zeke stood on the front porch waiting for them. As Ace parked the car, he quickly approached. Opening the passenger door, he held a hand out to Ali. When she shakily placed hers on his palm, he pulled her out of the car and into his arms.

"Before you talk, you should know, Daddy, that Ali and Jamie have past conflicts," Ace shared with his Daddy over Ali's head.

Zeke looked bewildered. "Who the hell is Jamie?"

Ali lifted her head to look at him in surprise. "Jamie! You were taking care of her in the kitchen. Putting a Band-Aid on her as if she was your Little!"

"I don't know what you thought you saw, but the delivery driver brought pizza again. This time she tripped over the edge of the sidewalk as she was handing me the boxes. My hands were full, and I couldn't catch her. She scraped up her hands and knee badly. I was only putting the Band-Aids on her because she couldn't do it herself. I don't know why she kissed me. You missed seeing me immediately push her away."

"Did you want her to be your Little girl?" Ali said, searching his face for any sign that he was deceiving her.

"Oh, Little girl. I am so sorry. I have not done a good job as your Daddy if you doubt that I wish for you and you alone to be my Little girl. Having met you, it would be impossible to continue searching for someone else." Zeke leaned down as if to kiss her, but he hesitated. "I love you, Little girl. I love Ace. You have become my entire life."

"You love me?" she asked incredulously. The worst day of her life seemed to have just become the best.

"Yes!" he whispered against her lips.

Ali rose on her toes the fraction of an inch to press her mouth against Zeke's. Wrapping one arm around his neck, she clung to him, never wanting to lose contact with his warmth. She reached her other arm out behind her toward Ace, inviting him to join them. When he enveloped her from behind, the most essential pieces in her world clicked back into place. She needed these two men.

When his lips lifted, she repeated the words back to him, "I love you, Daddy. I love Ace. Is it possible for us to be together again?"

Zeke ran a hand through her hair. Pulling her back up to meet his lips, Zeke kissed her passionately before responding, "I don't think I'm ever letting the two of you out of my sight again."

Meeting Ace's gaze, Zeke ordered, "Come here, Little boy." The older man drew Ace in for a kiss before adding, "Thank you for bringing Ali to talk to me. Your trust in me put our family back together."

Ali nodded her agreement. "Everyone always thinks Ace is the hothead and I'm the calm one. They don't know either of us very well."

"I want to know both of you better than anyone else in your lives. Will you come back in so we can make plans to visit SANCTUM?" Zeke asked, hugging them to his body as if he'd never let them go. He breathed out a ragged sigh of relief when both Littles nodded.

CHAPTER 14

Holding Ali on his lap, Zeke patted the cushion next to them, inviting Ace to sit close. The young man dropped onto the couch and laid his head on Zeke's shoulder. He gathered both of his Littles to him and hugged them close. Closing his eyes, Zeke sent a mental thank-you to everyone who might've helped. Squeezing Ace close to his body, he knew the Little had saved the trio.

"SANCTUM is about a two-day, hard drive from here. We don't want to go for a quick weekend visit. Would you be willing to come with me for a week?"

"A road trip could be fun," Ace said, sitting up to meet Zeke's gaze. His hand reached over to pat Ali's shoulder. "What do you think? Do you think the bar can exist without us there?"

"Yes," Ali answered simply. "I want to go see SANCTUM." She turned to meet Zeke's gaze. "What happens if we get there and we don't want to come back?"

"Then we don't come back. My SUV is large. Why don't we take those things that are most important to you with us? Anything we leave could be boxed up and sent to you later." Zeke studied both of their faces, trying to read their thoughts.

"I think the only thing I don't know that would fit in the vehicle is my surfboard. I'd hate to lose it," Ace admitted.

"I have a rack on my roof. We can tie it down with Ali's board as well. There isn't an ocean or waves, but there's a big beautiful lake," Zeke suggested.

"Ooh, paddleboarding! I always wanted to learn how to do that. I know they have paddles here. Could we take a couple with us?" Ali asked.

Zeke marveled at the change in his Little girl. She had gone from total devastation to happily snuggling on his lap. He had learned that her heart was fragile and that she would need frequent reminders of how much he loved her. Zeke would be glad to do this for her. "Of course."

"When will we leave?" Ace questioned.

"How about Wednesday? Do you think that will give the restaurant time to change its schedule?" Zeke probed.

Totally opposite from her personality, Ali declared, "They'll be fine. They survived without us for a long time." When Ace nodded to agree, Zeke knew it was time to make definite plans.

Ali borrowed Ace's phone to call the manager. After she'd broken the bad news to him, she handed over the phone so Ace could talk to him. He was definitely not happy as Ace disconnected the phone. The manager had warned them that anyone they hired to fill in at the bar could become a permanent employee. That would cut Ali and Ace's hours or replace them completely.

Each knew leaving now would destroy their life here. Ali nodded slightly at Ace, and he returned the signal. They would go for it. This was what they'd always dreamed of, and Zeke had become integral to their life. There wasn't anything holding them back.

Ace's stomach growled, making them all laugh. Zeke hugged them both to his body. Ace observed, "I guess pizza delivery is out." They all looked at the two pizza boxes Ali had dumped into the trash can as soon as they walked in.

"And we can't go to work," Ali pointed out.

"I want to celebrate. What's a fun restaurant that you've always wanted to try? Something not so froufrou that we have to dress up in a suit and tie, but a special place?" Zeke suggested. He could tell immediately that an idea had popped into the minds of both the Littles.

"It's kind of expensive..." Ali hesitated as her voice dwindled away.

"This is a celebration. Tell me what you thought of?" Zeke reassured her.

"We love sushi. It's super expensive for the good stuff, and Ace eats too much," Ali accused.

"Hey, I'm hungry. I can't help it if one of those little rolls doesn't fill me up," Ace protested. He looked to Zeke for his agreement.

"You're right. You are always hungry. I think I can afford a boat of sushi. Where's the best place?"

Raising his hands over his head, Ace waved them over his head as he celebrated. "Wahoooo!" Ali joined him by striking his hand in a high five. The celebration ended abruptly with Ace remembered Zeke's words. "You said boat. I've never had one of those big wooden boats filled with sushi. Can we get one of those?"

"That sounds like the perfect way to celebrate to me. What do you think, Ali?" Zeke asked.

Grinning from ear to ear, Ali bounced slightly on Zeke's lap. "I can't wait! Can we go now?"

Chopsticks clicking, Ace was ready when two waiters placed the sizeable wooden boat in the center of the table. They pointed out the types of sushi on each deck. Helping himself immediately, Ace chewed on his second helping as they finished. Zeke laughed when Ali stuck her tongue out at him.

"Manners, Littles. I'm sure neither of you wishes to go stand in the corner while we eat?" Zeke suggested. He laughed as they sat up straight and declared a truce.

An hour later, he drove back to the house with two sleeping Littles buckled in the back seat. Their stuffed tummies had lulled them into dreamland before he'd even hit the road that ran around the coast. Zeke's lips curved in a fond smile to discover that Ali snored while Ace slept as quiet as a baby. He had so much to learn about these two. Thank goodness, he had another chance.

. . .

The next day while they packed up the things they wanted to bring with them to SANCTUM, Zeke returned the rented surf board. Abe and Ashley still manned the store. Laughing, Zeke stepped around the young child as she had a tantrum in the middle of the store.

"Some days are more challenging than others, aren't they?" he asked Abe.

"You can say that again. Sounds like you're experienced with children," the shopkeeper commented as he indicated that Zeke should prop the board against the front counter.

"I'm learning more every day about Little ones," Zeke answered easily. "Thank your son for letting me borrow his board. It helped me find some special people."

"That's funny. My son tells the story of almost crashing into Ashley's mom when he was riding the board," Abe patted his granddaughter's head when she heard her name and ran over to hug his leg. "He swam to check on her, and the rest is history. He'll be home in four days on leave. I'm sure he'd like to meet you."

"Unfortunately, I'm headed back to my home tomorrow. Give him my thanks, please. That board is definitely lucky." Waving goodbye, he stepped back over Ashley, who had figured out the tantrum wasn't working and now played with the flippers on the bottom row.

CHAPTER 15

Driving through the immense gate that protected SANCTUM, Zeke rolled down the window to breathe in the beautiful country air. While Ali and Ace didn't grow up in a big city with smog and fumes, they were accustomed to the ocean's scent. "Take a deep breath, Littles. This is what wilderness smells like."

"I think I smell cows and horses, Daddy!" Ali protested, pinching her nose.

"Yep! That's the barn over there," Zeke confirmed. "Have you two ever ridden a horse?"

"No way! You have horses? Could I be a cowboy? Didn't you say that Nicky rides bulls? Maybe he could…" Ace didn't even get to finish that last suggestion.

"No way, Little boy. You will not be riding massive bulls bent on trampling you. I will, however, teach you how to ride horses if you wish. Your balance on a surfboard will help you sit properly on the beautiful creature."

"Fine." Ace reluctantly accepted the restriction.

"Look, there's someone over there! She's waving!" Ali pointed to the house just inside the entrance. There on a large deck stood a slender brunette. Ali stuck her head out the window to wave back.

"That's Shelby."

"Can we stop and meet her?" Ali begged. "I feel like I've been sitting forever."

"Me, too," Ace chimed in.

"Of course. Shelby loves greeting everyone." Zeke drove down the gravel drive to the sizeable house and tooted the horn as a greeting and to alert the Daddies that they were approaching.

Immediately, a large man with brown hair and an equally fit blond exited the house to join Shelby on the deck. They each captured one of her hands and held on to prevent their Little girl from racing off the wooden platform toward the moving car. Walking leisurely, they kept her safe until Zeke parked. Only then did they release Shelby's hands.

"Hi! Hi! I'm Shelby. Everyone is going to be so jealous that I got to meet you first," the friendly Little greeted them as they stepped out of the SUV. She dashed forward to wrap her arms around Ali first and then around Ace as well, surprising both the Littles. Sensing that, Shelby leaned forward to whisper confidentially in a voice loud enough to be heard by the three Daddies, "I hope you don't mind. Most Littles like to be affectionate."

"Hi, Shelby! Thank you for explaining. We have a lot to learn about being Little. We may need lots of advice," Ali reassured her quickly. Instantly, she liked the friendly, enthusiastic Little.

"Gosh, I'm sore!" Ace confided as he rubbed the stiffness out of his bottom.

"Me, too! I wouldn't finish my dinner because I ate too much popcorn. What did you get spanked for?" Shelby asked.

"I didn't get spanked..." Ace began when Ali chimed in, "Not this time. We're both sore from traveling from the coast."

"Do you all know how to surf?" Shelby asked, pointing at the boards lashed to the roof.

"Yes! Do you?" Ace asked.

"I've watched them do yoga on a board in the water on TV. I tried it at home and fell off the ironing board. Luckily and unluckily, my Daddy Jeremy caught me. I got more than a spanking for that mistake."

"Shelby, invite your friends in to have some cookies and milk with you. I'm sure they're hungry," the blond Daddy requested.

Shelby stepped forward and twirled around to stand between Ali and Ace. She held out her hands to them. "Come on! We can have our cookies in my nursery." When they placed their palms against hers, she darted forward, pulling them after her.

At the back door, a young dog greeted them. "This is BJs. He's the best dog in the world," Shelby explained before talking to the obviously besotted pet, "You can't come with us, BJs. Last time you ate all the cookies." She shook her finger reproachfully at the wiggling dog, who simply licked her hand in delight. Giggling, she ushered her new friends into the house.

"You have a nursery?" Ace asked as they walked through the kitchen.

"Of course! I love my nursery." Shelby led them down the hall. With a flourish and a ta-da, she escorted them into her nursery.

Ali and Ace looked around in astonishment. It was like something out of their dreams. Large, adult-sized versions of baby furniture filled the colorful area. An enormous chest stood against the wall. Toys of all varieties welled out of the top. Ali ran over to the crib and touched the satiny smooth wood before admiring the fluffy comforter and pillows inside.

Whirling, she asked, "Do you get to sleep here?"

"When I'm not sleeping with Daddy Beau or Daddy Jeremy," Shelby shared.

A sound from the hallway alerted the Littles that refreshments would arrive in seconds. "Come sit down at my table." When they hesitated to sit down again, she ran to the corner to get two large pillows to place on the seats. "That should be better. You can play with the stuffies that were in the chair. I had a tea party earlier for some of my friends."

When Ace and Ali sat with a sigh of relief for the soft cushions, she asked, "Would you tell me about yourselves? I love meeting new people."

"Could you start?" Ali asked, feeling nervous. She picked up a stuffed panda and hugged it to her chest.

"Sure! I'm Shelby. I met my Daddy Jeremy at the office where I used to work. Daddy Beau is his best friend. I'd always knew I was supposed to have two Daddies. That's what I'd always dreamed of. When I met Beau, he gave me those same tingles that had signaled that I belonged with Daddy Jeremy."

"Did I hear my name?" Jeremy's deep voice resonated from the doorway.

"The news has spread quickly! Rita and Nicky came over to meet you, Ali and Ace." He stepped back to allow them to rush into the nursery.

"Hey! Another Little boy!" Nicky announced, heading directly to Ace. "I've been smothered by girls here!"

In response to this outrageous statement, Shelby and Rita swarmed him and began hugging him. Shelby looked over her shoulder and motioned with her head for Ali to join. Immediately, Ali leaped forward to join the fun. Giggles filled the room as Jeremy indulgently watched from the doorway. He finally skirted the hugging swarm to set the tray of cookies and milk on the low table before shaking his head and leaving them alone.

"Save me!" Nicky waved his arms frantically toward Ace. Of course, Ace had to wade into the fray and became sucked into the mass hug. At last, they all collapsed to the floor, already great friends.

"Hey, cookies!" Rita pointed, and the party scurried to take chairs. Everyone wanted to sit next to Ali and Ace.

The hostess, Shelby, explained to the newcomers she'd just shared her story of meeting her Daddies. "Nicky, you go next. How did you meet your Daddy?"

"Boy wants to be a rodeo star. Boy meets a real rodeo star. A Little boy falls in love with rodeo star," Nicky summed up his entire relationship in three sentences before picking up a chocolate chip cookie and taking a monster bite while everyone laughed.

"I hate to follow that! Let me try… Hmm," Rita said before tapping her fingers against her lips. "Got it! Endangered girl hides in a horse trailer. Amazing Daddy rescues her. Little girl finds her true self and falls in love."

"Wonder if I can do that?" Ace proposed. "Let's see... Two best friends meet a handsome man at a bar."

"Bonding occurs over surfing and building sandcastles," Ali contributed.

"They visit SANCTUM as his Little boy and girl!" Ace crowed the final step.

"Are you going to stay?" Nicky asked the million-dollar question.

Ace and Ali looked at each other, trying to figure out how to answer that question. "We don't know. We love Daddy."

"Then you stay," Shelby announced for them.

"Is it that easy?" Ali asked, looking from one face to another.

"It is!" Rita and Nicky asserted at the exact same time.

"Jinx!" Shelby crowed before explaining, "Now, you can't talk until someone says your names three times."

Ace shrugged and ate a cookie. He and Nicky began talking in hand signals that they somehow understood. Nicky was offering to teach Ace how to ride a horse when he discovered that the newcomer had never tried. The latter returned the favor by pantomiming standing on a surfboard and paddling.

Nicky accepted that offer immediately.

"Rita, Rita, Rita," Shelby supplied. The girls wanted to talk to each other as well.

An hour later, Zeke stood in the nursery's doorway. The scene in front of him went straight to his heart. The Littles had pulled a fantastic array of toys from Shelby's toy chest and played what looked like three different games at once. Each chattered happily. Ali and Ace were definitely part of the group already.

Ace looked up to see him. Immediately, he jumped to his feet and ran over to hug Zeke. Stepping back, he shared, "Nicky's going to teach me how to ride a horse."

"That sounds like a lot of fun!" Zeke celebrated with him as Ali came to get a hug. Zeke kissed the top of her head before asking, "Are you having fun also?"

Ali nodded her head, enthusiastically. "Shelby's nursery is so much fun!"

"Do you think I could steal the two of you? I have something to show you."

"Can we come back to play another time?" Ace asked with hope shining from his brown eyes.

"I hope there'll be many playdates in your future," Zeke reassured him.

"Okay, Daddy!" Ali agreed.

"Go tell your new friends goodbye," Zeke encouraged, giving them a soft swat on the bottom when they turned around.

Giggling, Ace, and Ali held hands as they walked back to the group. After several rounds with hugs and promises to come back to play, they returned to their Daddy's side. "We're ready to go!" Ace informed him.

With final waves, Zeke guided them out to the SUV. Piling in, the Littles were full of stories to tell about their new friends. Driving down the secluded path to the home site he had chosen, Zeke enjoyed the obvious fun they had had at Shelby's house. Mentally, he hoped that the other Littles had given them one more reason to stay in SANCTUM.

When he pulled up in front of a large two-story cabin, the stories evaporated. "Wow! Is this your house? It's beautiful," Ali complimented, bouncing in place on the seat.

Zeke's eyes took in all the large and small touches that Charlotte Gordon had added to his house, making it home. Three rocking chairs stood on the porch, along with a large swinging platform equipped with a thick mattress. The latter would be perfect for taking afternoon naps in the fresh air. Hanging on the front door was a pink and blue wreath of flowers, and lacy curtains hung in the windows to lure them inside.

Ace tried to open the back door, but the childproof locks kept him inside. He flopped back against the seat and urged, "Come on, Daddy! Let's go in!"

Sliding out of the vehicle, Zeke opened the door, allowing them to join him. Immediately, the Littles ran to the front porch. Each claimed a rocker as Zeke followed at a more leisurely pace. They ran to join him at the door as he opened it. The group spilled inside to look around.

"This is beautiful!" Ali looked around in amazement.

Charlotte had outdone herself. Entirely decorated, the house was so close to what Zeke had imagined that he wondered if she was a mind reader for a brief second. This wasn't just a house—it was a home.

Room by room, the trio explored. In the kitchen next to a large oak table, two adult-sized high chairs stood ready, one draped with a blue bib and the other with a pink one. Between them, a regular kitchen chair for their Daddy. Ace ran to his and picked up the bib in amazement. "It's a dinosaur on the surfboard! And look, Ali! Yours is a unicorn!"

"Look!" Ali pointed to a small cup of something so familiar from home. Small plastic cocktail swords waited for them. Her giggles filled the room as Ace and her Daddy reenacted their great air battle.

Tearing them away from the welcoming kitchen, Zeke led the way upstairs. The master bedroom was enormous and filled with a bed more massive than anything they had seen before. It would be a comfortable size for a Daddy and two sprawling Littles. The attached bathroom had a gigantic triangular tub that would allow the three of them to take a bath together.

This time, Ali ran forward to pick up one of the bath toys lining one side of the tub. "Look at these! I think those are bubble bath!" she crowed, pointing to the bottles containing creamy liquid. "Can we take a bath?"

"There are a few more rooms here on this top floor. Let's go look at a special place before we empty the car and take a bath," Zeke suggested. He guided them down the wide hallway with a hand on their lower backs.

He paused at the door decorated with two names: Ace & Ali. "Who wants to open the door?"

Ace bolted forward to turn the door handle. Bursting through the entrance, he froze before reaching back for Ali's hand. Ace pulled her gently forward and wrapped an arm around her shoulders. The two Littles stood trying to take in everything in the room.

Two pale pink walls met two baby blue ones. Colorful bedding filled a crib for each of them. The changing table and dresser sat against one wall while the other held the huge, open toy box. Small details everywhere attested that Charlotte had designed this room especially for the two of them. It included an immense mural with three animals surfing: a Daddy bear, a unicorn, and a T-Rex with his arms stretched out for balance.

"Look out the window," Zeke directed. Immediately, they rushed to look out at the backyard. A huge square container filled with sand stretched under the window. They had their own sandbox to make castles forever. Ace turned to look at Zeke with an amazed expression.

Ali bolted back to throw her arms around Zeke's torso. She buried her head against his chest and sobbed. Ace followed her and cuddled up to his Daddy's side as Zeke and Ace comforted the Little girl. "Cheer up, Ali. This shouldn't make you feel sad!"

Raising her tear-stained face, Ali sobbed, "I'm not sad! I'm so happy! This is our room, isn't it? You really, really want us to stay."

Zeke tenderly wiped the tears from her cheeks. "I've wanted nothing else since the day I met the two of you at the bar. You're my Littles."

Ali looked at Ace, who nodded. The Little boy cleared his throat, demonstrating that he also had been moved by the beautiful room. "We don't want to go back. We want to stay here with you forever."

"We're so glad we found you, Daddy!" Ali added.

Zeke pulled them in close and hugged the two Littles tight against his body. "Welcome home."

CHAPTER 16

They unloaded the car rapidly, and Ali pulled her Daddy and Ace back to the huge master bathroom. After days of travel, a bath sounded like heaven. She sniffed each of the decanters of bubble bath before choosing one. "This one smells like bubblegum."

"Bubblegum bubble bath," Zeke repeated, looking at the ceiling in a silent thanks to Charlotte. Only a Little girl would know precisely what another Little would love. Uncapping the bottle, he poured a generous amount to the rising water. Immediately, a sweet smell of bubblegum filled the air.

Stepping to the Little boy's side, Zeke unfastened his belt and jeans before pushing his underwear and pants to the floor and slipping off his shoes. With a swat on the bottom, Zeke directed, "Ace, go potty while I get Ali undressed." During their time together at the coast, he'd discovered that managing two Littles required some coordination of activities. While the Little boy ran to the toilet, Zeke quickly removed all of Ali's clothing.

As Ace flushed the toilet, Zeke sent Ali to take his place. She hesitated until he also spanked her small bare bottom. Then with a giggle, she skipped to the potty, passing Ace on his way back.

Zeke stripped off Ace's T-shirt, socks, and shoes. Still kneeling before him, Zeke stroked his Little boy's penis, enjoying its instant reaction. "Now that we're here at home, you'll be my special Little boy. I arranged for something just especially for you. I'm going to wrap you carefully in a diaper."

He knew he'd suspected correctly when Ace's eyes darkened with desire. His Little boy needed to be taken care of completely. That didn't mean that he wouldn't resist.

"And Ali, too?" Ace demanded.

"Ali will wear a diaper when she has her period. But other than that, she's a bigger Little. She gets to use the potty on most days. But you, Little boy, are special. I need to take special care of you."

Ace launched himself forward to lean over to wrap his arms around Zeke's neck. He pressed a passionate kiss to his lips as a silent thank-you. When Zeke rose to his feet, Ace snuggled against him. "I love you, Daddy."

"I love you, too, my wild Little."

They stood wrapped around each other for several seconds until Ali rejoined them. The little girl eagerly pushed against each of them. "No hugging! It's time for a bubble bath. Look!" She turned and pointed at the filling tub. A massive mound of bubbles topped the steaming water.

Zeke ran to turn off the water with a laugh. "I can't lose the two of you in all those bubbles. I guess I must join you." He reached an arm over his head to grab the back of his T-shirt and pulled it off.

"We'll help you, Daddy," the two Littles chimed in together before running forward to help Zeke undress.

When he was nude, Zeke lifted Ali into the water and helped her settle on one side. Turning to Ace, he put his hands around his Little boy's waist. When Ace resisted, Zeke looked at him sternly. "Daddy's job is to take care of you, and your job is to be Little." Instantly, Ace stopped fighting to get away. Zeke placed him into the water and helped him sit in another corner.

Once Zeke joined them, their feet met in the center. Brushing each other with their toes, he discovered that they were both ticklish. Sounds of happiness filled the room as the Littles pulled their feet away. "Come here, you two," he invited, moving to the center of the tub.

Their slippery skin rubbed against him as Zeke hugged them close. An idea formed in his mind. Glancing around the room, he spied precisely what he needed. Charlotte had tucked a sturdy plastic stool under the counter for a woman to use as a makeup center. His Littles didn't need makeup, so he'd use that for a totally different purpose. "Daddy's going to grab something. Stay here."

Stepping out onto the thirsty rug, Zeke stood for a minute to let the water drip off. Then he dashed over to grab the stool. When he turned, he discovered his Littles decorating each other with bubbles. Ace now had a soapy shirt, and Ali had devil horns on her hair.

"Come on, Daddy. Play in the bubbles with us!" she invited, cupping a handful of the rich suds.

When he approached with his arms full, Ali playfully blew the bubbles at him and laughed when they stuck to his erection.

Setting the stool next to the tub, Zeke shook a finger at her. "Be careful, Little girl." Ali giggled and hid behind Ace.

"Don't put me in the middle of this!" Ace protested.

Zeke climbed back into the tub and lifted the plastic seat to place it in the middle of the tub. Immediately, the water threatened to overflow as the seat floated up. "Ali, come sit on the stool," he directed.

"Am I in trouble?" she asked, sinking deeper in the water.

"No, sweetheart. You're in for a treat."

"Okay!" Ali popped out of the water to sit on the stool.

The water dropped to an acceptable level. "What next?"

"Ace and I will make you a beautiful sculpture with bubbles. Strike a pose," Zeke instructed.

Immediately, Ali placed one hand on her hip and the other out like a spout. "I'm a little teapot."

"Perfect. Stay just like that." Zeke motioned to Ace to follow his example. Scooping up a handful of suds, Zeke smoothed them over one impudent breast. He deliberately brushed across the sensitive underside and rolled her taut nipples between his fingers as he adjusted the suds to just the right shape.

With a wink at his Daddy, Ace got to work decorating her other breast. The final result didn't matter much. Ali's eyes had closed to allow her to concentrate on the feel of their hands on her body. Ace slipped behind her to press kisses and bite the sensitive curve of her neck. He kissed her deeply when Ali turned her head. As if by magic, he made her pout disappear by touching his lips to hers.

Zeke nudged her legs apart and knelt between them. His fingers trailed down the center of her torso to trace the sensitive division of her labia. Ali spread her legs wider, inviting his touch with a gasp under Ace's lips. He was pleased to feel the slick arousal fluid that already coated her intimate folds. His fingers traced the delicate tissue before dipping into her tight channel.

"It stings, Daddy," she whispered.

"The bubbles can be harsh on a Little girl. Daddy will make it better." Signaling to Ace, he lifted Ali into his arms and moved the trio into the large shower. Zeke adjusted the water temperature and rinsed away the suds on Ali's body.

She spread her legs automatically as he moved the handheld showerhead between her legs. Ali could feel the jets of water pulsing against her clitoris and labia. Zeke rotated it slowly, washing away the sting and turning the water spray into an erotic treatment.

Ace set the stool in the center of the shower and helped Ali settle on the seat as Zeke sprayed his Little boy free of soap. Hanging the handset to spray warm water over their bodies, Zeke ensured that his Littles would not become chilled. He planned to be there for a while.

Zeke moved between Ali's thighs and held her gaze as he sank to his knees before her. She swallowed hard, and he felt his lips part in a half-smile as he watched Ace move behind her. Ali looked over her shoulder as he knelt behind her. Ace captured her lips in a fierce kiss that twisted her body, presenting one breast to Zeke. He accepted that invitation and closed his lips around her beaded nipple.

Ali arched her torso in pleasure as two sets of hands caressed her body. Zeke released her breast with an audible pop. Kissing a trail down her chest, he traced her inner labia. A gush of arousal from his Little girl made his explorations easier. Glancing up, Zeke found that Ace's hands now caressed her breasts as he nibbled on her sensitive neck.

"Hold on," he whispered, guiding one of her hands to his shoulder before pulling her hips over the edge of the stool. It now supported her body completely. Desire darkened her blue eyes as her gaze rose to meet his. Holding her attention, he lowered his mouth to the private areas between her thighs. Zeke felt her fingernails dig into the muscles of his shoulders.

"Mmm!" he hummed against her sensitive tissues as he tasted her sweetness. One lick would never be enough as he explored her body. Her flavor was addictive. His finger brushed lightly around her vaginal opening as his lips sucked softly on her clitoris. Her hips automatically lifted toward him, inviting more. Taking care of her, he slid two fingers into her tight channel to answer her silent plea.

Glancing up her displayed body, he discovered that her fingers were now wrapped around Ace's erection. She stroked it with practiced delight as she held him close with a hand at his waist as he tantalized her breasts. His fingers quickly became soaked with her juices.

When her Daddy stood, Ali protested, "Daddy, don't stop," as her eyes flew open to watch him. He opened a small compartment out of the spray of water in the shower stall to remove a small packet. She watched him roll it onto his thick shaft. As he returned to his knees, Ali whispered, "Yes, Daddy. Please!"

Ace's hands over her drenched hair reminded her of his presence. A wicked thought flew through her brain. Leaning her head back, she met his eyes and deliberately licked her lips in a silent invitation. Need hardened his face, pushing her desire even higher as he moved closer. Ali gripped his hips with her hands to pull him close.

A deep moan of arousal burst from her core as her two men began to enter her body. Their thickness stretched her body, bringing her double the pleasure. Her Daddy lifted her legs over his shoulders to render her completely helpless. Unable to lift her body, Ali used her tongue and internal muscles to lavish irresistible sensations on her men.

Their bodies crashed together. Watching their faces, Ali's heart clenched inside her chest as Zeke leaned forward, pulling Ace's mouth toward his for an aggressive kiss. With that voyeuristic push, her body exploded into a massive orgasm that tensed her entire body. The men both shouted, and the sound ricocheted against the slate tile lining the shower walls. Memorizing that sound, Ali never wanted to forget the echo of the pleasure she had helped bring them.

Later, lying in bed together, Ace raised his head to ask, "Daddy?"
"Yes, Little boy?"
"Do we have any food here? I'm hungry." The roar of his empty stomach made everyone laugh.

"Let's go see. We'll have to stock up on food. There's no pizza delivery out here," Zeke teased before kissing his sweet Little girl.

"Thank goodness," she answered when she could talk again. "Thank you for finding us, Daddy," she added in a soft whisper that Ace repeated loudly.

"You are the lights of my life. Thank you both for helping SANCTUM become our new home. I love you!" Zeke kissed both Littles, cuddled close to his body.

Another rumble from Ace's stomach almost drowned out their sweet, "I love you," but Zeke heard them. Damn, he treasured these two! *Forever.*

EPILOGUE

Zeke stood on the large stone patio, looking out over the lake. He had chosen this location to build his house because he'd always loved the sound of water. Now, he appreciated this decision every day. His Littles were definitely water babies. Their home had become a gathering spot for the Littles at SANCTUM on scorching afternoons.

Jeremy's hand landed hard on his shoulder. "It looks like they're settling in well," he commented.

"Better than I could ever have imagined," Zeke answered.

The two men stood watching the antics of the Littles in the water. The collection of two surfboards had grown to five paddleboards. Whether they were being used for water yoga, races across the lake, or lazy sunbathing, the boards were always in high demand. The Daddies were ever vigilant to make sure everyone was safe and playing nicely.

"Daddy! Make Ace stop splashing water on us!" Ali demanded, pointing an accusing finger at the young man using his paddle to launch water over Rita, Priscilla, and herself.

"They started it! The girls moved right in our racing lane," Ace protested.

Hunter and Nicky backed him up with a supportive "Yeah, they're in the way."

"Ali, Ace, meet me on the dock." Zeke excused himself and walked across the back lawn to the large wooden dock that extended into the water. He was pleased to see his Littles didn't argue but immediately paddled back to meet him.

Pulling each up on the solid surface, Zeke helped Ali and Ace secure their boards so they wouldn't float away. "Hugs first!" Zeke ordered. His Littles loved each other so much, but sometimes it was necessary to remind them to protect the relationship over meaningless squabbles. A smile curved the corners of his lips as he watched the two wrap their arms around each other. When they turned to look at him, snuggled next to each other, Zeke could tell that the argument was already over. He stepped forward to kiss each of them on the forehead.

"It's almost time for your naps." Zeke talked over their protests that they weren't sleepy and that they could have fun and play together nicely. "Shelby's Daddies brought over cookies. Would you swim out to invite your friends to come in for a snack?"

The mention of a sweet treat erased all arguments. Grinning at each other, his two Littles took off at a run and dove into the water. Zeke watched them swim across the lake like fish. He had worried that they would miss surfing in the ocean, but his Littles had adapted well to the smaller body of water.

As each Little arrived on the patio, their Daddy stripped off their wet bathing suit to send them into the large outdoor shower. When they'd rinsed the lake off their skin and out of their hair, each Daddy wrapped them in a large towel. Each Little had quickly abandoned their self-consciousness to be exposed in front of the group. The other Littles didn't care what they looked like, and the Daddies were just taking the best care of them.

"Go potty, Ali," Zeke directed, noticing his Little girl's dancing feet. Ali couldn't wet on the fish in the lake any more than she had been able to pee in the ocean. Wrapping his arm around Ace, Zeke helped him lie down on one of the padded mats to be wrapped in his diaper.

"Do it, Daddy," Ace begged.

Winking at him, Zeke pressed his lips against his Little's tummy and blew, making a funny noise. Immediately, the other Daddies tried to outdo him as all the Littles giggled at the weird sensation. When Ali raced to his side, not wishing to miss the fun, Zeke opened her towel and repeated the action.

Zeke hugged his two tightly against him. His dreams of having a Little boy and a Little girl had come true. A Daddy couldn't ask for anything more.

When all the Littles had gone home, Ace's favorite time of the day began. He loved playing with his friends, but nothing could top time with his Daddy. Ace no longer felt silly lying across his Daddy's lap as he drank a warm bottle before his nap. He wrapped his hand around the strong one holding the yummy formula.

His Daddy smiled at him, and Ace knew that he understood. SANCTUM had become his safe place. Ace treasured time with his beloved Ali and now with the man who had helped his fantasies become real. The one who didn't laugh at his need to be taking care of and cherished.

His Daddy had created rules and guidelines for him. Although he spent a lot of time in the corner and had trouble sitting on a hot bottom, Ace knew that his Daddy loved him and wanted the best for him. He was happier than he'd ever been before.

Ali hugged her stuffie to her heart. Tucked into the soft bedding of her crib, Ali listened to the whispers of her two favorite people in the world. Her Daddy would rock her when she woke up. She loved lying on his broad chest with the pacifier in her mouth as she woke up slowly.

Zeke was always vigilant to spend alone time with both of his Littles. Ali thrived in his care. She'd gotten used to taking a nap and going to bed early. Although she hated to admit it, she felt better than ever. Ali clenched her small bottom, feeling the slick lubricant and the thick anal plug. Her Daddy was intent on making sure that she was healthy. He treated her bottom regularly to make sure that she would enjoy their sexual encounters fully.

She enjoyed taking a nap with her bottom filled. Her Daddy would reward her when she sat on his lap to wake up. His thrilling touch brought her pleasure as she had never imagined. He knew what she needed to feel so good. Closing her eyes eagerly, Ali allowed herself to drift off to sleep.

THE END

EXCERPT FROM THE MAGIC OF TWELVE: ROSE

Rose was dragging by the end of the day. Her caffeine-fueled body had hit severe deprivation mode two hours ago.

At least it was finally time to leave, she thought as she clocked out and waved at the boss in his office. She owed Sam Kaprik. He'd given her a job out of mechanic's school when other shops wouldn't even look at her credentials.

Not fitting the profile of a heavy-duty mechanic, most owners scanned her five foot and a half-inch, thin frame and laughed. She could read their thoughts, "No way this scrawny girl can handle working on those big trucks." They were wrong, of course, but only Sam had been willing to give her a chance. He'd also created an atmosphere in the repair bays to prevent most of the hassles the other mechanics might throw her way.

Given time, Rose had demonstrated just how strong she was. Or at least, how good she was at problem-solving and using her resources to attack any obstacles her size caused. She'd worked hard to avoid asking anyone for help with the tasks required by her job, but was always available to pitch in if someone else called for assistance. Now, the other mechanics sought her advice when facing something out of the ordinary.

She'd also cloaked her feminine side. By always wearing baggy coveralls with big T-shirts underneath, her small curves disappeared. The men had quickly stopped trying to look down her shirt or check out her ass. There wasn't anything to ogle.

"Hey, Little sis! See you tomorrow. Bring more coffee. You need it," one mechanic yelled after her as she walked through the open garage doors.

"Not the kind of Little I want to be," Rose grumbled to herself as she dragged her depleted body to her car.

Hoisting herself onto the high bench seat, Rose started the ancient truck she relied on since she was sixteen. "Come on, Big Blue. Let's go home," she suggested as she turned the ignition. Smiling as the powerful motor purred like an expensive supercar, Rose shifted it into gear and pulled out of the parking lot.

A glance in the rearview mirror revealed a grease smear across her forehead. The drive-through attendant would have to ignore it, Rose thought as she steered the old behemoth to a coffee shop. She'd never make it home without some caffeine.

Five minutes later, she took the first sip. "Yesss!" she hissed in appreciation of the hot brew. Life looked a bit better than it had since she'd dumped her coffee that morning. Now, second-guessing herself, Rose was sure she must have placed it on that shelf. Who'd mess with her coffee? She didn't have any enemies.

One block short of the duplex she rented, red lights and the blare of a siren sounded behind her. Automatically, she steered the truck to the curb, expecting the patrol car to pass her. Despite the powerful engine, Rose never sped. There wasn't anything waiting for her at home. She didn't need to hurry.

To her surprise, the cruiser pulled to the curb behind her. Puzzled, Rose rolled down the window before placing her hands on the steering wheel. She knew she didn't look dangerous, but being a cop was a tough job. She didn't want to cause any problems. Besides, she was sure this was a simple mix-up.

Watching in the mirror, she could see the officer talking on his radio. *What is going on?* Seconds later, two more marked police vehicles appeared and boxed her truck into the curb. Each patrolman got out with their hands on their weapons.

Those wiggling wires popped into her head. T R U S T N O O N E ! Rose began to panic. She had done nothing wrong. They couldn't have her truck mixed up with any other vehicle. No one else drove a car this old.

"Get out of the truck with your hands where we can see them," the shouted instructions sounded tense as if the police officer was worried.

"Officers, I don't understand what's happening. I have done nothing wrong," she assured them as she tried not to panic.

"Out of the truck, now," a different patrolman ordered.

"Okay!" Leaving her keys in the ignition, Rose pulled the latch to open the heavy door and pushed it open.

"Keep your hands where we can see them!"

Slowly, she lifted her hands and began to slide off the high seat. The heel of one work boot caught on the frayed carpet by the door, and she grabbed desperately at the door to steady herself. Swinging from an arm draped through her open window, Rose froze as clicks sounded. The safeties were off, two of the handguns pointed at her.

"Sorry! I'm okay. Look!" she dropped to her feet and raised her arms back over her head. "My hands are up!"

Within seconds, her chest was roughly pressed against the hood of the nearest patrol car. Metal cuffs were tightly closed around her wrists before they stood her up to frisk her.

"What's going on? What did I do?" she asked, her voice shaking with fear and bewilderment.

"Is that the cop-killer they've been reporting about all morning on the TV? She doesn't look very dangerous," an elderly woman's voice asked.

"Go back inside, ma'am. We have this all taken care of now," one officer called. Looking back at the other policemen, he gripped, "Looky loos! They've been watching all morning as we tracked this bitch. Dispatch has gotten all sorts of false reports. Now that we've got her, they don't think we've got the right one."

"Wait! You don't have the right one! I've been at work all day. I haven't killed anyone. Call my boss. Call Sam Kaprik at Diesel and Semi Repairs," Rose begged urgently.

"Yeah, I'm going to get right on that," the officer commented sarcastically as he jerked her from the hood. "Move." He shoved her roughly to the back door of the squad car and yanked open the door. When Rose hesitated in the open doorway, he pushed her into the seat. Kicking her work boots into the car, he slammed the door.

This can't be happening! Wedging her feet against the floor, Rose pressed herself up to seated. She watched the patrolmen high five each other before radioing in that they had apprehended the shooter. Their excited voices easily heard through the closed windows.

Rose looked desperately around to see if anyone would help. Now the neighbors had all ventured out onto their lawns. Pointing phones her way, Rose knew that she was being recorded. She would never live this down at work.

Follow Rose's story today on Amazon!

AFTERWORD

If you've enjoyed this story, it will make my day if you could leave an honest review on Amazon. Reviews help other people find my books and help me continue creating more Little adventures. My thanks in advance. I always love to hear from my readers what they enjoy and dislike when reading an alternate love story featuring age-play. You can contact me on
my Pepper North FaceBook page,
on my website at www.4peppernorth.club
eMail at 4peppernorth@gmail.com
I'm experimenting with Instagram, Twitter, Pinterest and MeWe. You can find me there as well!

For your reading enjoyment, my other age-play stories are:

DR. RICHARDS' LITTLES

A beloved age play series that features Littles who find their forever Daddies and Mommies. Dr. Richards guides and supports their efforts to keep their Littles happy and healthy.

Zoey: Dr. Richards' Littles® 1
Amy: Dr. Richards' Littles® 2
Carrie: Dr. Richards' Littles® 3
Jake: Dr. Richards' Littles® 4
Angelina: Dr. Richards' Littles® 5
Brad: Dr. Richards' Littles® 6
Charlotte: Dr. Richards' Littles® 7
Sofia and Isabella: Dr. Richards' Littles® 8
Cecily: Dr. Richards' Littles® 9
Tony: Dr. Richards' Littles® 10
Abigail: Dr. Richards' Littles® 11
Madi: Dr. Richards' Littles® 12
Penelope: Dr. Richards' Littles® 13
Christmas with the Littles & Wendy: Dr. Richards' Littles® 14
Olivia: Dr. Richards' Littles® 15
Matty & Emma: Dr. Richards' Littles® 16
Fiona: Dr. Richards' Littles® 17
Oliver: Dr. Richards' Littles® 18
Luna: Dr. Richards' Littles® 19
Lydia & Neil: Dr. Richards' Littles® 20
A Little Vacation South of the Border
Roxy: Dr. Richards' Littles® 21
Dr. Richards' Littles®: First Anniversary Collection
Jillian: Dr. Richards' Littles® 22
Hunter: Dr. Richards' Littles® 23
Dr. Richards' Littles®: MM Collection
Grace: Dr. Richards' Littles® 24
Tales from Zoey's Corner - ABC
Steven: Dr. Richards' Littles® 25
Tales from Zoey's Corner - DEF
Sylvie: Dr. Richards' Littles® 26
Tami: Dr. Richards' Littles® 27
Liam: Dr. Richards' Littles® 28
Dr. Richards' Littles®: 2nd Anniversary Collection
Tim: Dr. Richards' Littles® 29
Tales From Zoey's Corner - GHI

Once Upon A Time: A Dr. Richards' Littles® Story
Tales From Zoey's Corner - JKL
Tales From Zoey's Corner - MNO
Tales From Zoey's Corner - PQR
Serena: Dr. Richards' Littles® 30
Tales From Zoey's Corner - W, X, Y, Z
Tales From Zoey's Corner - A-Z
Sophie: Dr. Richards' Littles® 31

SANCTUM

Pepper North introduces you to an age play community that is isolated from the surrounding world. Here Littles can be Little, and Daddies can care for their Littles and keep them protected from the outside world.

Sharing Shelby: A SANCTUM Novel
Looking After Lindy: A SANCTUM Novel
Protecting Priscilla: A SANCTUM Novel
One Sweet Treat: A SANCTUM Novel
Picking Poppy: A SANCTUM Novel
Rescuing Rita: A SANCTUM Novel
Needing Nicky: A SANCTUM Novel
Adoring Ali & Ace: A SANCTUM Novel

THE KEEPERS

This series from Pepper North is a twist on contemporary age play romances. Here are the stories of humans cared for by specially selected Keepers of an alien race. These are science fiction novels that age play readers will love!

The Keepers: Payi
The Keepers: Pien
The Keepers: Naja

The Keepers Collection

THE MAGIC OF TWELVE

The Magic of Twelve features the stories of twelve women transported on their 22nd birthday to a new life as the droblin (cherished Little one) of a Sorcerer of Bairn. These magic wielders have waited a long time to take complete care of their droblin's needs. They will protect their precious one to their last drop of magic from a growing menace. Each novel is a complete story.

The Magic of Twelve: Violet
The Magic of Twelve: Marigold
The Magic of Twelve: Hazel
The Magic of Twelve: Sienna
The Magic of Twelve: Pearl
The Magic of Twelve: Violet, Marigold, Hazel
The Magic of Twelve: Primrose
The Magic of Twelve: Sky
The Magic of Twelve: Amber
The Magic of Twelve: Indigo
The Magic of Twelve: Rose

Other Titles
The Digestive Health Center: Susan's Story
Electrostatic Bonds
Perfectly Suited
The Medic's Littles Girl
3rd Anniversary Collection
Tex's Little Girl
Marked Brides

ABOUT THE AUTHOR

Pepper North is a hybrid author whose contemporary, paranormal, dark and erotic romances have won the hearts of many loyal readers. After publishing her first book, Zoey: Dr. Richards' Littles 1 on Amazon in July 2017, she now has over fifty books and collections available on Amazon in four series.

She is one of Amazon's Most Popular Erotic Authors, rising to number one in the top 100. She credits her success to her amazing fans, the support of the writing community, and her dedication to writing.

- amazon.com/author/pepper_north
- bookbub.com/profile/pepper-north
- facebook.com/AuthorPepperNorth
- instagram.com/4peppernorth
- pinterest.com/4peppernorth
- twitter.com/@4peppernorth

Made in the USA
Coppell, TX
29 May 2024